**DANNY YUKON**
**and the**
*Secrets of the Amazing Lamp*

To: Marshawn Lynch

Thanks for being you my ninja! Keep grindin
& never stop shining. And keep making a
difference in the world, I see you working
with the youth. Proud of you bruh.
                    Much respect & love,

**Danny Yukon and the Secrets of the Amazing Lamp**
by Prince Daniels, Jr. with Pamela Hill Nettleton
Copyright © 2014 by Prince Daniels, Jr. with Pamela Hill Nettleton

Illustrated by Liza Biggers
Cover Designed by Siori Kitajima, Sf AppWorks LLC
http://www.sfappworks.com
Formatting by Siori Kitajima and Ovidiu Vlad for SF AppWorks LLC
E-Book Formatted by Ovidiu Vlad
Cataloging-in-Publication data for this book is
available from the Library of Congress.

ISBN-13: 978-0-9916629-5-1   ISBN-10: 0991662954
E-book published by The Sager Group at Smashwords.
info@TheSagerGroup.net   info@MikeSager.com

# DANNY YUKON and the Secrets of the Amazing Lamp

by Prince Daniels, Jr.
with Pamela Hill Nettleton

illustrated by Liza Biggers

THE SAGER GROUP

Artifex Te Adiuva

To the co-creator K.K. Sadhaka, thank you
for the inspiration. Love is eternal.

For Q.

# contents

# chapter ONE

*C*rack!

The snap of the bat hitting the ball was crisp and clear in the late summer air.

"Run, Stephen!" yelled Stephen Fishman's father, jumping to his feet in the bleachers behind home plate.

From the dugout with the rest of his team, Danny Yukon watched Mr. Fishman shake his left fist in the air, his hotdog in his right hand forgotten. It slipped to a sharp angle and bright yellow mustard dripped onto Mr. Fishman's new white running shoes. Mr. Fishman never noticed. "Go, Stephen! Go!"

Danny cheered with his teammates. "Run, Fish, run!"

Next to Danny, Shawn Dunn hopped up and down and whistled. His black glasses jiggled to the end of his nose and fell off.

Rachel Julia Poplaski scooped them up and tossed them over to Shawn who caught them with barely a glance, his eyes riveted on Fish rounding second base.

That's just how they work together in the infield, too, thought Danny. RJ scooped up balls and threw them fast as a wink to Shawn; Shawn tagged first base and the runners were out.

Twigs Tanner shook his head in appreciation and spit a pink wad of gum down into the dust at Danny's feet. Remember not to step on that, Danny told himself.

"Here he comes!" yelled Shawn, still bouncing, his eyeglasses threatening to hop off the end of his nose again.

"A home run," whispered RJ, her hands clasped under her chin. That was RJ all the way, thought Danny. When something really mattered to her, she got very quiet.

"Attaboy, Fish!" Twigs bellowed. Twigs always bellowed. Danny didn't think he had ever heard Twigs do anything but bellow when he spoke.

But the Dundee Drummers, a darn dopey name for a baseball team if ever he heard one, thought Danny, had a left fielder with a strong arm and a shortstop who could think fast on his feet. The ball and Fish hit home plate in a cloud of dust and cheers and hooting.

"You're...out!" yelled the umpire, whose mask and cap and chest protector made him look like a leather turtle. In real life, the umpire was just Tony Rojas who ran the little grocery store across from the Lincoln Middle School. At Rojas's, there were 17 different flavors of gum and licorice in the shape of pinwheels. Danny had two red ones stuffed deep in the pocket of his windbreaker.

Fish was face down, pounding the dirt with his fist. The score was 3-2. They had lost the last game of the summer to the dumb Dundee Drummers.

Shawn hung his head, and this time, his glasses did fall off again. For the second time that afternoon, RJ picked them up. She patted Shawn on the shoulder and looked over at Danny.

"C'mon, guys," she said. "Let's go shake hands."

"Trying out for football?" asked Shawn. He slipped off his baseball cleats and reached for his running shoes.

"I dunno," said Danny, digging his toe into the dirt. "I'm better at baseball." But he wanted to be better than anyone else at football.

"They let us play with the seventh graders, so a few guys on the team will know what they're doing."

"I can't wait!" bellowed Twigs. "We're gonna work out with the team every day! We're gonna sweat 'til our shoes are squishy!"

RJ rolled her eyes. "*Such* an impressive skill," she said.

It really is, thought Danny.

Shawn tied his shoes and grabbed his cleats with one hand. "Headed for the parking lot?"

Danny shook his head. "Naw...you go on ahead. I'm gonna sit here a minute."

"And think deep thoughts about life?" yelled Twigs. Twigs's breath smelled like bubble gum and cheeseburgers.

"Twigs," said RJ, "you have the manners of a two-year-old."

And the breath of a drive-thru, thought Danny.

"You going out for football, RJ?" asked Twigs.

"Man, you know girls don't play football," said Shawn, looking nervously at RJ.

RJ just grinned. "Girls *do* play football, Twigs," she said. "Just not on your team. Which I would do if I felt like it."

"You got that right," said Shawn, dodging a punch in the arm from RJ.

"I'll leave the sweaty shoes to you," said RJ. "During the school year, it's just me and my cello."

"Just you and your Jell-O?" blurted Twigs.

"Cello. Cello, you idiot." RJ pretended to step on Twig's foot. "It's a musical instrument, not a food."

Shawn nodded. "She's awesome on that thing. She can play 'Star Wars'."

Shawn gave Danny a gentle poke in the shoulder. "You okay, Danny?"

"No worries," said Danny. "No big deal. Just sitting."

Shawn nodded. RJ opened her mouth to speak but Shawn shook his head. RJ nodded silently and Danny's two best friends walked behind the bleachers to the waiting cars of their parents.

Twigs shoveled dirty socks, his extra baseball cap, and his battered mitt into a ripped gym bag. "See you in school on Monday, Yook."

I hate it when you call me that, thought Danny. But he supposed Twigs wasn't very fond of his nickname, either—even if his legs were as long and as skinny as two toothpicks.

"See ya, Twigs," said Danny.

Twigs swung his gym bag up over his shoulder and marched off toward the bleachers. Then he stopped and turned around. "Hey, Yook!" he yelled.

Maybe he wasn't yelling, thought Danny. Maybe he was just speaking normally, for Twigs, but even far away, it sounded like yelling.

"Hey, Yook! Come on out for football tryouts. Monday after school. Squishy shoes!" Twigs waved wildly. Danny lifted one hand and waved slowly.

Squishy shoes, he thought. Yeah, right.

When the voices of mothers calling "Hi, honey!" and fathers saying "Let's go get ice cream, Sport!" faded away and it sounded as if all the cars had left the parking lot, Danny climbed the three steps out of the dugout and brushed off his uniform pants.

He ambled slowly toward the bleachers, the parking lot, and the long walk home, tossing his mitt up in the air and catching it.

He made up a little rhythm in his head and tossed the mitt up on every third beat.

> *Squishy shoes*
> *Squishy, squishy shoes*
> *Squishyshoes squishyshoes*
> *Squishy sho-sho-shoes*
>
> *Squishy shoes*
> *Squishy, squishy shoes*
> *Squishyshoes squishyshoes*
> *Squishy sho-sho-shoes*

Could a football player really sweat so much that his shoes got soggy? Danny wondered. Did it have to happen specifically to shoes? Could you get, for instance, squishy elbows? A shoulder? A kneecap?

> *Squish-ee ELBOWs....*

Naw, that didn't work at all. Back to shoes.

*Squishy shoes!*
*Squishy squishy shoes!*

"Yo, Danny!"

Danny caught his mitt and looked to his left. A pale gold station wagon slowed down on the street.

"Hey, Fish," said Danny. He bent down a bit to look in the window. "Mr. Fishman."

"You don't have a ride, young man?" asked Mr. Fishman.

Danny wanted to invent a wonderful answer that would make Fish and his father go away, but he just couldn't think of one. "My mom is late," he said, finally.

"Climb on in, son," said Mr. Fishman. "We'll drop you at home."

"Oh, no thanks, Mr. Fishman," said Danny. "I'm happy to walk." But Mr. Fishman had already opened the door to the back seat, and Fish was waving Danny over.

The back seat and the way-back seat behind him were piled with lamps. Table lamps. Office lamps. Little lamps. Big lamps. Lamps with leopard shades. Lamps with striped shades.

"Lamps," said Danny. And then felt like an idiot.

"Lamps," said Mr. Fishman, grinning widely. "I sell lamps."

Fish nodded from the front seat. "Not out of the car, of course," he said. "Dad has a shop downtown."

"On the weekend, I drive around and buy lamps at garage sales, yard sales, flea markets…just about any-where you might find a lamp!" Mr. Fishman chuckled as if that was the funniest thing a man could ever say.

"Lamps," said Danny again. "Lots of lamps."

"Lots!" Danny could see Mr. Fishman's face reflected in the rearview mirror. Maybe Mr. Fishman never stopped smiling.

Mr. Fishman reached across the front seat and set his big, freckled hand on top of Fish's head. He ruffled Fish's sandy hair.

"Nice play at second base today, fella," said Mr. Fishman.

Fish looked over at his dad and grinned. Those Fishman men sure did like to smile, thought Danny.

"I'm proud of you, son," said Mr. Fishman.

Suddenly, Danny's throat felt as if he couldn't swallow or breathe. His eyes started to burn.

Mr. Fishman caught Danny's eye in the mirror. Quickly, Danny looked away, out the window, into the yards and gardens of the houses they passed in the car. Count the houses, he told himself. Count them! So he did: four, five, six...stop sign...seven, eight...He told himself to breathe, just breathe, and pretty soon, he felt like he could breathe again. Nine, 10, 11...almost home.

Danny held up his mitt, pretended to examine the stitching in the glove, and, his face blocked from Mr. Fishman and his mirror, wiped his eyes with his fingers.

Danny wanted to tell Mr. Fishman to drop him off right here on the corner, that he didn't have to drive up to the door. Danny wanted out of that car, fast. But he didn't trust himself to try to speak, so he let Mr. Fishman drive.

"You say hello to your mother for me, will you?" Mr. Fishman's eyes were in the mirror again.

Danny nodded. He took a breath and managed to squeak out "Yes, sir." Danny pulled up on the handle and the door swung open.

Danny set one foot on the driveway.

"Danny?" No more mirror. Mr. Fishman turned around and looked right into Danny's eyes. "Your father misses you, son. He is being very brave."

Danny nodded quickly and shut the door behind him. He ran around the side of the house to the back door.

Hidden by the house, Danny sagged against the back fence and took a shaky breath.

Mr. Fishman shifted his car into reverse and backed out of the driveway. He looked over at his son. For once, Mr. Fishman was not smiling.

"Danny's father is being very brave," he told Fish. "And so is Danny."

# chapter TWO

"You didn't tell me your team had a game this afternoon." Danny's mother spread chunky peanut butter on one slice of bread and creamy peanut butter on another. With a long-handled fork, she speared a dill pickle from a jar and set it on the cutting board in front of her. She lifted a knife to begin slicing the pickle into round coins.

"No, no, no!" From his kitchen chair, Danny lifted a hand to stop her. "The long way, the long way!"

Danny's mother smiled, turned the pickle on the board, and sliced it lengthwise into three strips. As she arranged them on the creamy peanut butter, she raised one eyebrow at Danny. "The game?"

Danny took both pieces of bread from her and carefully pressed them together. "You had to work, anyway," he said. "You couldn't have come."

His mother reached over his shoulder with a knife and cut the peanut butter and pickle sandwich in two, from corner to corner.

"Did I get that right?" she asked.

"Perfect," said Danny, and took a bite.

"But had I known about it, I could have at least felt guilty," she said. She kissed the top of his head. "Oops. Peanut butter. Hold still."

Danny froze, his sandwich halfway to his open mouth. "Mom!"

"So I snuck a taste!" She said, laughing. She turned to the sink, wet a paper towel, and turned back to his hair. "Just about got it…"

Danny looked longingly at his sandwich, suspended over his plate. "I didn't tell you about the game because I knew you couldn't make it," said Danny. "I didn't want you to feel bad."

"So you made yourself feel bad. Oh, honey."

"I know you'd be there if you could, Mom."

"I know you know," she said. And kissed the top of his head again. "You're sure you don't mind getting up so early for Dad? Big day tomorrow. You could use your rest."

Danny had a mouthful of chunky and creamy peanut butter, so he just shook his head "no." Talking to his Dad was worth waking up at 4 a.m. Even if it meant he'd be sleepy on the first day of school.

4 a.m., no call.

4:30 a.m., no call.

5 a.m., no call.

5:15—wait! "Mom!" The Skype ring chimed on Mom's computer.

Danny's mom had fallen asleep on the sofa waiting for the call from Afghanistan.

She shrugged off the heavy red throw Grandma had crocheted when Danny was just a baby and ran over to the desk where Danny sat, waiting in front of the computer monitor.

"Did you get back to sleep, hon?" she asked him.

"Too excited," said Danny.

The picture flickered on the screen. And there he was. "Dad!"

"Little man!"

"David." Danny's mom smiled her biggest smile, the one that made her eyes crinkle. "He's at least a *medium*-sized man by now."

Danny's father grinned and winked at Danny.

"You look tired, hon," said Danny's mom.

"Commo blackout the last two days—I was waiting by the Internet tent this afternoon hoping for the blackout to lift. I coulda used a nap." Danny's father wore khaki-and-tan camouflage fatigues. A sewn-on patch over his pocket read "YUKON" in capital letters. On the other side, over another pocket, another patch read "U.S. ARMY." Danny thought when his dad's hair was cut this short, his ears look even bigger than usual. And Dad had some big ears.

"You've had trouble?" Mom's voice sounded tight and worried.

"A communications blackout," said Danny. "That means someone in the battalion was killed and nobody can call home until the family's told, right?

Danny's father rubbed a long-fingered hand over his face and sighed. "How many companies in this battalion, soldier?"

"Five, sir," said Danny.

"That's hundreds of troops. Hundreds. And in any town of hundreds of people, now and then, someone has an accident or gets hurt. Just like home."

"But sometimes someone gots shot or gets blewed up, right?" Danny asked.

Danny's dad almost laughed. "I don't even want to try to mess with *that* grammar. Tell me about school."

"I don't know anything yet," said Danny. "I don't catch the bus for the first day for another two hours. But I can tell you about the bus. Last year's bus was *stinky*. I don't what ever happened on that bus, but man—"

"Okay, chatterbox, slow down," Dad smiled. "Sorry to wake you up early, bud."

"No problem, Dad."

Danny's dad reached into his pocket. "I didn't forget." He pulled out a folded piece of paper. "Check this out." He held up a square of newsprint in front of his computer's camera and unfolded it.

"Dad! Awesome!"

"David, that's really lovely."

"My two Daniels," said Danny's dad.

"Gramps and me," said Danny.

"Gramps and you," said Mom to Danny. Turning to the screen, she said, "I'm glad you can still find time to sketch, honey."

Danny's father shook his head. "This place," he said. "It's either crazy, non-stop, no-sleep, or so boring I draw pictures in the sand."

"I'll hang it next to the other ones," said Danny.

"I'll mail it today," said Dad. "Write me about school, ok?"

"Sure, Dad, will do."

"Gwen, I only have another minute or two…"

Danny's mom kissed Danny's cheek. "Danny, how about you try to sleep for another hour before school? Let me talk to Daddy for a minute, peanut."

Danny rolled his eyes at his father. "Mush, huh?"

Danny's father winked. "A little mush, yes sir. See you next time, son."

When he got to the door of the living room, Danny turned around to wave. His mother was resting her cheek on one hand. She reached out with the other to touch his father's face on the screen.

Love you, Dad, thought Danny. Bye.

The alarm was sharp and angry.

Dang! thought Danny. I was just about to take off! He slapped the snooze button and closed his eyes again.

I was just on the football field. The quarterback handed off the ball and I grabbed it. A giant linebacker tried to tackle me. No way! I spun past him. A cornerback dove to the grass and grabbed my ankles. His hands were huge! I danced away. My feet were flying. I ran and ran. If I could make it to the end zone—just past that orange pylon—they couldn't get me. I felt the wind on my skin. I felt my feet pound the ground. Oh no! A safety with big, strong shoulders that bunched and stretched as he ran was headed straight for me. Through his helmet, I could see that his teeth were clenched tight. He was going to hit me! The only way I could score was to—jump! I lifted off and tried to fly the three yards left between the end zone and me. I held the ball out as far as I could stretch. Flying! Flying, fly—

"Time to get up, sweetie!" yelled Mom. "You don't want to miss the bus!"

School! School. The first day of school. The new Levi's Mom just bought. The red Air Jordans he had begged for all summer. His favorite white Polo shirt.

As he did every morning, Danny stopped to look at the six drawings hanging on his wall. Every first day of school, Dad drew him a new one. Kindergartener Danny and mom, sitting on the front step, laughing. First-grader Danny and his new bike. Second-grader Danny and Dad, tossing a ball back and forth on the side lawn. Third-grade Danny trying to draw a picture himself. He liked that one. A drawing of a drawer drawing a drawing. Fourth-grader Danny playing with Shawn's dog, Pickles. Fifth-grader Danny wearing Dad's army hat and saluting. The sixth-grader drawing of Gramps with him would look great right there, in that space between the window and the door. Danny looked around the room. By the time he graduated from high school, the walls would be covered!

His favorite breakfast.

"Thanks for the oatmeal, Mom."

"No prob, kiddo. But you don't get the brown sugar kind again until your birthday."

"I'm reading the box here, Mom. It doesn't have *that* many calories."

"It's not the calories, kiddo, it's the sugar. Add in the hot chocolate. *And* the marshmallows. It's the sugar, sugar."

Danny laughed. "Dad would like that one."

"Bus in 10."

"Why is 'breakfast' two words stuck together?" asked Danny. "'Break' and 'fast.' That doesn't really make sense. If I was inventing a word for breakfast—"

"You're your father's son, that's for sure, always wondering about how words work. Now stop chattering on and go brush your teeth, or you'll be late." Danny's mom lifted his empty bowl off the table and steered him into the bathroom. "Ask Daddy about that when he gets home."

Danny popped back out of the bathroom, toothbrush in his mouth. "Mmmppt whee me uma rff rff?"

"Take your toothbrush out of your mouth, young man."

"Oops," said Danny. "Sorry, Mom. Will he be home for my birthday?"

"They don't tell him when, honey, they don't tell him. But I know he'd like to be." Danny's mom handed him his backpack and wiped his cheek off with a kitchen towel. "Toothpaste Face."

"Mother of Toothpaste Face."

"Son of the Mother of Toothpaste Face." Danny's mother opened the back door.

"I know, I know, don't tell me," said Danny. "Don't be noisy at the bus stop. Don't stand on Mrs. Caperton's prize dahlias. Say hello to the bus driver. Don't believe everything the kids say about how crabby my new teacher is."

His mother kissed the top of his head. "I am shocked," she said. "You've been listening to me again. Throws me off my game."

Danny ran for the bus like the linebacker and the cornerback and the giant safety with the clenched teeth were all after him. He sprinted to the rose bush. Cut over to the clump of white daisies. Headed for the willow tree as if it was an orange pylon at the end zone.

And jumped right over Mrs. Caperton's prize dahlias.

# chapter THREE

**D**anny shot off the school bus and raced to the side-walk clutching his books like they were a football and he was an NFL running back. Two fourth-graders blocked his path. A hop and a turn and he was past them. Charlie Ferris raised his hand to wave. Danny waved and zigzagged left and then right. Was that RJ up ahead? Danny ran for the stairs and was sacked by Principal Rasmussen putting a hand on his shoulder.

"Walk, Mr. Yukon," she said.

"Yes, ma'am," said Danny meekly, and walked through the front doors of the school.

"Danny!" bellowed Twigs from the hallway. Danny waved.

"Danny!" called RJ. "We're in the same room!" She stood outside Room 103, reading a list of student names. "Mr. Moore!"

"He's so cool!" said Shawn. "I've got Mrs. Wilson."

"No biggie," said RJ. "It's just for homeroom. We move around from room to room for the rest of the day. I bet we have at least one class together."

"I hope it's algebra," said Shawn. "I suck at math. And you don't!" He gave RJ a gentle punch in the arm. She gave him a punch right back.

"Ow!" said Shawn.

"Weenie," said RJ, leading Danny into their homeroom.

Danny looked back at Shawn and grinned. "See you at lunch, weenie."

Three periods later, Shawn, RJ, and Danny did find themselves in the same class, but it wasn't math. It was geography.

"This year, ladies and gentlemen, we will look at Europe, Asia, and the Middle East," said Ms. Albright.

"Including Afghanistan?" wondered Danny. RJ shot him a shocked look, and Danny realized he must have said that out loud.

But Ms. Albright didn't get angry. "An excited student!" she said. "Now I'm excited, too!" She walked halfway down the row of desks and stood near Danny. "Do you know a little bit about Afghanistan, Danny?"

RJ rolled her eyes.

"A little bit," said Danny.

"A big bit, Ms. Albright," said RJ.

Ms. Albright smiled. "You up for a challenge, young Mr. Yukon?"

Danny grinned and nodded.

Ms. Albright looked up at the ceiling for a moment and tapped her chin with her pencil. She looked back down at Danny with a twinkle in her eye.

"How large is Afghanistan?"

"About the size of Texas," said Danny.

"Which ocean does it border?"

Danny smiled. "None. It's landlocked."

"She's tricky," whispered Shawn to RJ. The kids in the class turned around to watch Danny duel with Ms. Albright.

"How many countries surround landlocked Afghanistan?"

Danny thought back to a day before his father had been deployed, to a map his father had showed him. He counted in his head. "Five. No. Six," he said. "Six."

"How many people live in Afghanistan?"

"Thirty million," said Danny. Ms. Albright looked impressed.

"Thirty million, plus his dad," said RJ.

Shawn nodded. "Plus his dad."

"Your father's there," Ms. Albright said. "In the military?"

"He's an Army," said Shawn.

"No, he's a troop," said RJ.

"He's a troop in an Army," said Shawn.

"But he'll be coming back soon," said Danny.

"When he does," said Ms. Albright, "Maybe he would come to class with you and tell us *all* about Afghanistan."

Danny smiled. This was going to be a very good school year!

Sloppy joes, tater tots, and cole slaw.

"My favorite!" yelled Twigs.

"Everyone in the entire cafeteria heard you," said RJ, unwrapping her bagged lunch that her father had packed. RJ's father was just about the healthiest person Danny had ever met. Mr. Poplaski probably never ate a candy bar or a cookie. Heck, he probably just pulled grass up out of the lawn and ate it, thought Danny.

"You're just jealous because you can't eat a bun," grumbled Twigs.

"You're just jealous because you wish you had my gluten-free sandwich!" said RJ.

No one wants your gluten-free sandwich, thought Danny. He dipped a tater tot in ketchup.

"Ew," said Shawn. "Ketchup?"

"It's kinda like a french fry," said Danny.

Shawn stared at the tater tot in his hand. "I guess..." he said, though he didn't sound too sure.

Twigs grabbed Shawn's hand and shoved it down into the ketchup. Shawn shook his hand free and flicked ketchup all over the table. RJ rolled her eyes.

Shawn lifted a dripping, soggy, ketchup-logged tater tot to his mouth and then suddenly stopped, tater tot dripping rhythmically on the table. Shawn's eyes were wide.

"Now what?" RJ asked him. "You look like you just saw—" and then she followed Shawn's gaze to behind Danny's head.

Shawn's mouth hung open. Ketchup dripped. Danny, unaware that anyone stood behind him, just keep eating.

RJ coughed politely.

Danny looked up and saw Shawn. "Breathe, man," said Danny. "You look sick or something."

Shawn just kept staring beyond Danny's head.

Finally, Danny turned around.

Juliet Browne. The closest thing the Lincoln Middle School had to a movie star. She had the longest hair of any girl in the school, and when she danced ballet in the school talent show last year, she had tied it back with a pink, shiny ribbon. She was taller than any other girl, too, and taller than most of the boys. She always wore tiny little pearl earrings that dangled on silver wires, and her dimples flashed in her cheeks, even when she wasn't smiling. Sun from the cafeteria windows touched her brown curls and made a golden glow around her face. She looks like a fairy princess, thought Danny.

And then she spoke.

"Hi, Danny," she said.

Danny swallowed. It seemed to make a very loud noise.

Juliet smiled. Her dimples were glorious.

Danny swallowed again, and wondered if he had ketchup on his face. "I didn't think you knew my name," he said, in a small voice.

Juliet's eyes twinkled. "After Ms. Albright's class today, everyone knows your name," she said. "You sure are smart about Afghanistan."

Danny wondered if he should stand up. No. He'd have to untangle his legs first. "Yeah," he said. I sure am smart, he thought. So smart, all I can think of to say is "yeah."

"Later!" Juliet giggled, twirled, and was gone. The sunlight hit Danny in the eyes and he couldn't see. It seemed as though she had magically disappeared into thin air.

"Wow," said Shawn.

"Juliet Browne knows your name, Yook!" yelled Twigs.

All the nights Danny's dad had taught him about Afghanistan, all the hours he and his mom had studied the maps online, it had never occurred to Danny that anyone else would think what he was learning was interesting, or cool, or made him special.

"You *are* smart about Afghanistan," said RJ. Sometimes it seemed that she could read Danny's mind.

RJ took a bite out of her rather gross-looking gluten-free sandwich, and sighed. "That girl's never had a bad hair day."

Danny rested his forehead against the cool window of the school bus. Homeroom with Mr. Moore was lucky, and RJ was there, too. Geography with Shawn *and* RJ— that was great. And Juliet Browne actually *speaking* to him—that was more than cool.

Everything was new. Every room, every class, every teacher. Some of it was exciting. Some of it was, well, a little scary.

That geography class with Ms. Albright was fun today, but then Danny thought: What happens when we're not studying the Middle East anymore and class is about some place I've never even looked up on a map?

Mr. Moore in homeroom *was* cool. Shawn had been right about that. Mr. Moore was funny, and friendly, and having RJ in the same homeroom made it somehow more...homey. Danny smiled. A homey homeroom. He should remember to tell that to Mom. She would say something like, "Just like your father, always playing with words."

The bus slowed, its brakes creaking and groaning. Why were school bus brakes so noisy? Danny wondered. *Really* noisy. Noisier than Twigs Tanner, even. Hey, that was a good one. He should tell RJ.

Danny lifted his forehead off the glass and looked around the bus. Back at school, he had seen RJ climb on with her friend Mandy. Where were they sitting?

Not on the left side—not with Carl White and Jake Butler sitting over there, shooting spitballs at all the girls.

Danny swiveled his head. Not behind him, either.

"Hey, Yukon," said Charlie Ferris, with a friendly grin.

Danny nodded. "Charlie."

Must be up in front, then. Danny craned his neck to see over the head of Tony Cole, who was somehow much taller sitting down than he seemed to be when he was standing up.

Ah! There, third row from the front. He could see RJ's rainbow-colored headband. Danny took in a breath to whistle their signature whistle—two woots and a wheet—when the bus turned the corner onto Central Street, and Danny could see his house through the windshield.

Viewed from here, it looked far away, he thought. All the way to the front of the bus, then through the windshield, over the orange hood of the bus, down to the street, over the curb to the sidewalk, and up to the back of the big, black sedan parked just in front of the driveway.

Odd car, thought Danny. None of the neighbors drove a car like that.

As the bus lurched past his house up to the corner bus stop, Danny saw his front door open, his mother's arm holding it ajar. A man in an Army uniform stepped out in dress greens. His posture was very straight. Danny's dad was big on that. "Stand up straight, son," was something he said about a hundred times a day. When he was home with them, anyway.

A second man stepped out, this one with his hat in his hand. He turned to face back into the house, and Danny got a quick glimpse of his mother's face before the bus brakes squealed again. Her face looked…wrong.

The bus doors opened, and Danny was somehow standing at the top of the stairs down to the road. He didn't remember walking down the aisle of the bus.

And then he was on the sidewalk, watching the two Army men walk to their car. One turned to the passenger side, one to the driver's door.

Charlie Ferris pounded on the bus window, waving madly. "Your backpack, man!" he yelled. "Danny, you forgot your backpack!"

Danny's mother looked tiny, two houses away, at the door. But Danny knew she saw him, watched her hand rise to her mouth, saw her look quickly at the men as the black car pulled away from the curb.

And then Danny ran for home.

Right over Mrs. Caperton's prize dahlias.

# chapter FOUR

The tiger was white and the night was black.

The paws of the thing were immense, plush as velvet, soft and silent.

It watched Danny with a sly look in its eye. I know you're there, it seemed to think. I know just where you are.

The tiger's shoulders bunched and stretched with each step. It covered ground swiftly, almost flying, fast as the wind.

Then it turned its giant head toward Danny and opened its jaws.

Red. And teeth. So many teeth.

Danny screamed.

His bedroom door swung open and his mother was there. Her hair was damp and smelled like her flowery shampoo. He buried his face in her wet curls that smelled like a girl and held on.

Danny stared at the brown sugar oatmeal and hot chocolate with marshmallows. He didn't want to pick up the spoon.

Grandma Evie pulled a chair up next to Danny.

"Your Mama tells me this is your favorite."

Danny nodded. "It is, Grandma. Thank you."

"Used to be your Mama's favorite, too. Course I made it from scratch back then, no such thing as these little packets of nonsense." Grandma Evie slid the oatmeal box out of the way. "Come on, now, child. You eat."

Danny liked how Grandma Evie talked. The words came out all lazy and slow, but her eyes were quick and sharp as a bird, Daddy used to say to Mom. Gwen, your mother's eyes are sharp as a bird, he would say.

"Sharp as a bird," Danny said softly.

"What's that, young man?" Grandma Evie's long fingers played with the end of his spoon.

Danny wasn't sure Grandma Evie was thinking of feeding him herself, but maybe she was. She could be pretty bossy.

He lifted the spoon but it felt so heavy. He set it back down in the oatmeal.

Grandma Evie looked out the window a while.

"Gonna be a long, hard day," she said, almost to herself.

Danny pushed the spoon around in the oatmeal. "What do I have to do?" he asked in a small voice.

Grandma Evie kept looking out the window, but her hand reached under the table and took Danny's hand.

"You feel that, grandson?" she asked.

Grandma Evie's hands had skin like old paper. You almost thought they'd make a crinkly noise when you touched them, but they surprised you. They were strong. And warm.

"Uh-huh," whispered Danny.

"How about we just do that all day, then," she said.

Uncle Bucky tied Danny's tie, "a real tie, a man's tie," he told Danny. Uncle Bucky looked like Gramps, and Gramps looked like Daddy.

Gramps took a soft, white handkerchief out of his own suit pocket and handed it to Danny. Danny could never remember Gramps giving him anything. Gramps was a little scary: tall, loud, and sometimes angry-looking. When Gramps talked, even rooms away, everyone in the house heard him. Dad used to say that Gramps never needed a telephone—he could just stand on the front porch and talk and everyone in the neighborhood would hear him.

"You're a young gentleman now," said Gramps. "You carry that."

All the people in church stared at them. Danny didn't like that. Uncle Bucky said it was a sign of respect for Danny's father, and to not feel nervous.

Grandma Evie never let go of Danny's hand.

The cemetery was a long drive from the church. Longer than a walk, longer than a bike ride. Danny had never been in this part of the city before.

How can I visit him here? Danny wondered. I'll never be able to find this place again.

He was a little squished against the door in the back of the funeral home limousine. Grandma Evie was busy with Mom. Uncle Bucky and Gramps were talking softly. Gramps's eyes looked very wet. The car drove slowly through the cemetery.

Danny rested his forehead on the cool glass of the backseat window. He didn't like looking at the headstones and the grass, but up, up and over the tops of the trees, he could see the very top floors of St. Luke's Hospital, the tallest building near his house. Too far to walk, but at least he could see a little piece of home.

The limo slowed and then stopped.

Danny turned to look out the small back window and saw a line of cars, all stopping and parking behind them. Danny liked cars. He remembered who drove what. He and Dad used to make a game of that. RJ's family in the brown mini-van. Fish and Mr. Fishman in that gold station wagon. Danny hoped all those crazy lamps still weren't in the back of it.

The doors opened and grownups began to slowly climb out of the car.

"Miss Evie," said Uncle Bucky, offering Grandma Evie his arm.

Mom leaned heavily on Gramps. Gramps looked a little bit like Dad, just from the back, thought Danny. He put his arm around Mom's shoulders, just the way Dad had done.

Danny clambered out, and Grandma Evie took his hand.

Ahead, up there near the biggest tree, were soldiers. A flag.

And Dad.

Yesterday, when Danny said he'd never been to a funeral before, Uncle Bucky had made him a list. In pictures.

Bucky opened Dad's old sketchpad to a blank page.

"First, we dress up to honor the person who passed," said Bucky, drawing a little picture of a man in a suit.

"Why's that honor anybody?" asked Danny. "Who cares what we wear?"

"Do you dress up for school?" asked Uncle Bucky.

Danny thought about that first day, his new Air Jordans, and his favorite Polo shirt. "Yeah," he said.

"Well, why do you do that?" asked Uncle Bucky. "Why don't you just wear your pajamas?"

Danny smiled, imagining Fish and Shawn and Twigs at school in their pajamas. "We'd look dumb."

"What's dumb about pajamas? They're comfy."

"But they aren't right for school," said Danny. "School is where you learn, not where you sleep."

"Good," said Bucky, shading in the suit on the little man he had drawn. "So...why did you bother with the nice clothes on the first day of school? I mean, besides wanting the girls to think you looked fine." Bucky gave Danny a little shove on his shoulder.

"I like school," said Danny. "I want to look like I'm good at it."

"You respect it," said Uncle Bucky.

"Yeah, I do," said Danny.

"You respect your father," said Uncle Bucky.

"Of course," said Danny.

"You respect his work."

"I do," said Danny.

"Then we wear suits and we dress and act correct," said Uncle Bucky.

Danny nodded.

"Second, our friends and our family come to show us they love and support us and that they cared about the person who passed." Uncle Bucky drew lots of little people around the little man in the shaded-in suit. "That can be hard, because sometimes you might not want to talk. Sometimes, you might not want people to see how sad you are. That's okay, though. They love you. So just try to remember why they are there."

Uncle Bucky made curly ringlets of hair on one of the little people he had just drawn.

"Is that RJ?" asked Danny.

Uncle Bucky squinted at it. "Could be," he decided.

"What's third?" asked Danny.

Uncle Bucky drew a roof over the heads of all the little people on the page. "Third is that we're quiet in church, because that's the thinking time."

"What are we thinking about?" asked Danny.

Uncle Bucky looked a little sad just talking about it. "Your dad. We remember your dad."

"What do you remember, Uncle Bucky?" asked Danny. "About dad."

Uncle Bucky stopped drawing for a moment and tapped his pencil on the sketchpad. "Your dad always could draw better than me," he said. "And faster. He could eat faster, too. Sometimes he beat me to the best parts of your Grandma Bess's chicken."

"Dad stole your food?" asked Danny.

Uncle Bucky smiled a little smile. "Well, let's just say he got to it quicker than I could."

Danny smiled a little smile, too.

"See, now? It's nice to remember things together, isn't it?" asked Uncle Bucky. "So that's number four. After church, we all come back to the house, and we talk and remember." He drew little sofas and chairs around the people.

Danny thought about that for a moment. "Will I hear a lot of stories about Dad?" he asked.

"You will, indeed," said Uncle Bucky. "Some pretty good ones you've never heard before, I'm guessing."

"You forgot one," said Danny. "Before four. We go to the cemetery and there are soldiers."

"You're right," said Uncle Bucky. But he had stopped drawing. "I don't know so much about that part. I've never been to a military funeral before."

"What's different?" asked Danny.

"Hm..." said Uncle Bucky. "Well, there will be soldiers in uniforms, I guess."

He drew hats and boots on two of the little men.

"I don't think that's right," said Danny. "They would wear dress uniforms, not fatigues."

"See what you know all about that I don't?" Uncle Bucky bumped his shoulder up against Danny's again.

"The soldiers are an honor guard," said Danny.

"I like the sound of that," said Uncle Bucky.

"And there will be a flag."

Uncle Bucky began to draw the Stars and Stripes.

Six soldiers in the sharpest, most handsome uniforms Danny had ever seen stood in formation.

They marched and turned together. It was almost like a slow, fancy dance.

A big flag covered the coffin. The soldiers carried it from the hearse, a car that looked like a big station wagon, over to the trees. There were chairs there, and the pastor of the church.

As the soldiers passed, other soldiers saluted.

"That's for your dad," whispered Uncle Bucky. "They are saluting your dad."

People Danny didn't even know stood up very straight, the way Dad would have liked. And they saluted.

"Long ago, they were soldiers, too," said Uncle Bucky.

Regular people saluted, too. People who weren't wearing uniforms. But they stood up straight, as if they might have worn uniforms once. Gramps. Mr. White, who lived down the road. And Mr. Fishman.

# chapter FIVE

The tiger was back.

It ran, and ran, and ran. It seemed to be running away from Danny. For a moment, Danny felt safe.

But then Danny saw that it was really running straight at him. At him, and at him, and it wasn't going to stop.

The tiger smiled. Danny was afraid of it, and the tiger was glad.

Its rear legs dug into the ground.

Its front legs lifted.

There were claws.

Danny screamed.

Mom tried to talk softly when she spoke to Grandma Evie on the phone, but Danny could hear her if he held his breath.

"It's every night now, Momma," she said. "Danny doesn't sleep for more than two, three hours before he wakes up with another one of those nightmares. I don't know what to do for him."

Mom's voice sounded strange. Tight and worried. She used to sound like that sometimes when she talked to Grandma Evie about Dad being gone for so long. About Dad not calling or writing in a while. About missing Dad.

Mom said "uh-huh" and then "hm" and then not much for a while. Grandma Evie could talk for a long time without stopping.

When Mom finally clicked her phone off and set it down on the kitchen table, she sat still in her chair, looking out the window into the dark.

Fish was at the door.

Danny heard the doorbell and looked out the upstairs window. Down on the street, he could see Mr. Fishman's gold-colored station wagon. In the bright, morning sun, it looked pale, not gold at all, but almost white. Through the car window, Danny could see Fish's baseball glove sitting on the front seat.

"Danny!" his mother called from downstairs.

Danny really liked Fish. Danny liked Mr. Fishman, too. But for some reason, he did not want to see Fish, which was odd, because Fish was a good friend. Danny did not want to say hello to Mr. Fishman. Danny did not want to see either one of them today.

"Danny!" his mother called again.

He had to go downstairs. There was no way around it.

Mr. Fishman stood inside the front door, speaking softly to Mom. His white running shoes had a faint yellow stain from the dripped mustard during the big game with the Dundee Drummers.

Fish was outside the screen door, tossing a ball up in the air and catching it in the same hand. That was an old Fish trick; he did that anytime he got bored during practice.

"Dude," said Fish, when he saw Danny.

Danny swallowed hard and nodded.

Mr. Fishman smiled and reached his arm out to Danny's shoulder. Danny had two thoughts. One was to run back upstairs. The other was that if Mr. Fishman kept looking at him with that gentle look on his face, Danny might burst out crying. So he pulled away from Mr. Fishman and stood behind his mother.

"Danny!" said Mom, surprised.

"It's all right, Gwen," said Mr. Fishman.

"Danny, Mr. Fishman and Stephen wonder if you'd like to go play catch in the park," said Mom.

Fish pushed his face against the screen. He showed the ball to Danny. "C'mon, man!" he said, excited. And then, as if he remembered something, more quietly: "I mean—if you want to." Fish and Mr. Fishman exchanged a glance.

Danny wanted to go. Playing catch with Fish was always fun. Playing catch with Mr. Fishman might have been fun or dumb, who knows? But his feet felt rooted to the floor behind Mom as if he couldn't move.

"Danny's spent the last few days inside," said Mom. "It's so kind of you to ask him to play with you. It would be good for him to get out." Mom gave Danny a gentle nudge and smiled encouragingly at him. "Honey, it really is okay," she said. "Go. Enjoy yourself a little."

Enjoy himself? That seemed like something that would never happen again, with Dad gone, and never coming home. Danny didn't know what to do. He couldn't think of what to do. He couldn't imagine what to do. So he turned his face away from the visitors and leaned against his mother.

Puzzled, she shrugged.

"It's all right," said Mr. Fishman. "And Danny—" He spoke to the back of Danny's head. "Danny, we play catch almost every day. We'll ask you again. And if you find yourself in the mood, well, you just call up Fish and we'll hit the field."

The sound of Fish throwing and catching the ball stopped, and the screen door creaked. Fish walked around Danny's mother so he could see Danny's face. "I miss you at school, man," he said. "Are you coming back soon?"

Danny looked up into the face of his friend, and knew that Fish was being kind. I'll come back to school pretty soon, Danny thought to himself.

He opened his mouth to say that.

But nothing came out.

The new Levi's Mom just bought. The red Air Jordans he had begged for all summer. His favorite white Polo shirt.

It was almost like the first day of school, all over again.

"You're sure you're ready?" asked Mom. "If you'd like to stay home a few more days, I can call Mr. Moore and explain. I'm sure he'd understand."

Danny shook his head no.

Mom kissed him on top of his head. "Okay, peanut. You give it a try." She handed him his lunch. "And just call me if you want me to come pick you up. No shame in that. We'll try again another day."

Danny walked slowly to the bus. She didn't think he could do it. Danny wasn't sure he could do it, either.

In homeroom, Mr. Moore didn't say anything—just patted Danny on the shoulder when he walked in.

The other kids whispered to each other. Watched Danny take his seat. And looked at him strangely. At least, Danny thought they did.

In the hallway, Juliet Browne looked at him with sad eyes and no dimples. Twigs didn't bellow hello, he just gently punched Danny on the arm. No one was acting like usual. They were trying to be kind, but they made him feel like he wasn't like them anymore. All he wanted was to be the same Danny he had been just weeks ago.

In geography, Ms. Albright gave him a big smile. "I have your make-up work in my desk drawer waiting for you, Danny. Can you stop by right after school to get it?"

Danny nodded yes.

Then class began, and Ms. Albright projected a map of the Middle East onto the screen on the wall. "Today, we'll review what we studied last week," she said, lifting a long wooden stick. She pointed on the map here and there, asking questions.

"The Arabian Sea!" said Shawn, answering a question Danny couldn't remember hearing Ms. Albright ask.

Danny didn't want to listen. He didn't want to hear the word "Afghanistan."

"Syria, Iraq, and Saudi Arabia!" said RJ, answering another question Danny never heard.

Well, those three countries certainly were not Afghanistan. And the map Ms. Albright was projecting was one Danny and his mother had looked at together a hundred times. He had studied it with Dad, too, but he didn't want to think about that right now.

Right now, he wanted to think about what he knew about the Middle East. How many religions? Lots, including Christianity, Islam, and Judaism. Plus some others Danny couldn't remember, but he knew where to look them up. How many languages? Lots, too. Turkish. Arabic. And the two carpets…oh, yeah. Persian and Berber. He had to think of the white-colored rug in RJ's basement TV room to remember that one. Where is Egypt? In northern Africa, right across the Red Sea from Saudi Arabia. What's the big river? The Nile. And the Persian Gulf, that was where the oil was. All around the Persian Gulf. Danny decided to try to listen. It was distracting, thinking of these lists of things he knew. It helped him focus; it helped him think of something else for a minute or two. And he really wanted to think of something else. He didn't want to think of riding the school bus home to see those two soldiers coming out of his house, and Mom looking like—

"Can anyone name the canal that runs from here—" Ms. Albright tapped the Mediterranean Sea. "—to here?" She tapped the Red Sea.

Easy. The Suez Canal, thought Danny.

Like he was reading Danny's mind, Shawn said, right out loud, "Danny will know that!"

RJ turned to look at Danny. Shawn turned to look at Danny. So did Charlie Ferris and Jake Butler. Everyone was looking at Danny. Including Ms. Albright, who had a little frown line between her eyebrows. She seemed to be trying to decide something. Then she asked him: "Danny?"

Danny knew the answer. The Suez Canal. He even thought he might be able to remember how long it was—more than 100 miles, he knew that much for sure. The Suez Canal. The Suez Canal. The Suez Canal.

Ms. Albright smiled at him.

Danny tried to smile back. The Suez Canal. The Suez Canal.

From across the aisle from him, RJ whispered to Danny. "Pssst! What are you *doing?*"

Doing? Thought Danny? What does she mean, what am I doing?

Then he looked down at his hands. He was folding and folding a piece of notebook paper over and over itself until it turned into a fat triangle. Just like the way the soldiers folded the flag at the funeral.

"Danny?" asked Ms. Albright.

He opened his mouth. He wanted to tell her. He wanted to answer the question. He wanted to say, easy as anything, "Suez Canal."

But he could not make a sound.

The tiger opened its mouth.

Four long, sharp, pointed teeth, like fangs. Black lips. A red, red tongue.

And it spoke.

"Boy, who will be your protector now?"

Its roar shook the bed, shook the house, shook the earth.

Danny wanted to yell, to scream, to roar back.

He took a deep breath, planted his feet, and opened his mouth.

Nothing. Nothing. Nothing.

# chapter SIX

"He just won't go to school, Mama," said Mom into the phone to Grandma Evie. "Sure, he can still learn, but he can't ask questions. He can't answer questions. He can't talk to the other students. He feels embarrassed."

Danny took his time putting his dinner plate and fork into the dishwasher so he could eavesdrop on Mom.

"The doctor still isn't sure, Mama," she said, her back turned away from the kitchen. Her voice got quieter, but Danny could still hear her. "There's no physical reason, no physical problem. They can keep doing tests, but—"

Mom listened for a while, and Danny hovered in the kitchen.

"Yes, every night, the nightmares," said Mom. "Every night he wakes up screaming."

There was a long pause, now. Grandma Evie must be talking, in that slow, patient way of hers.

After a while, Mom shifted in her chair. Danny heard her say, "Maybe," very quietly. "Maybe you're right."

Her voice sounded strained. "Oh, Mama," she said, even more quietly.

In November, RJ sent a letter in the mail. A real letter, written in her tidy handwriting on school notebook paper, folded into an envelope that had a smear of something—peanut butter?—near the flap.

She wrote in pink ink. Danny had to hold it near the light to be able to read it. "Dear Danny. You've missed so much school that I forget what you look like. Ha ha! Let's go see a movie over winter break. Shawn sneezed hard in geography class and his glasses flew off and landed on Juliet Browne's desk. Ms. Albright had to pick them up and hand them back to Shawn. His face was so red! Speaking of red, I think Shawn has actually started to like tater tots with ketchup. Twigs and Fish got in an argument in homeroom about who is the fastest football player ever, and Fish is so quiet and Twigs is so loud that it sounded like Twigs was just talking to himself! It was really funny. We have a homework project: write a story about the hardest thing you ever had to do. Shawn is writing about learning to tie his shoelaces! Do you believe him? See you soon. I hope. —RJ"

Shawn's glasses landing on Juliet's desk. I just bet his face was red, thought Danny.

Mom appeared at the door of his room. "Nice of Rachel to write, huh?"

Danny nodded.

Mom stepped into Danny's room and kissed the top of his head. "Give yourself a little time, bucko."

Danny looked up and raised one eyebrow.

"You'll talk when you're ready to talk," she said.

But Danny saw the worry in her eyes.

Fish and Mr. Fishman were at the door again. This time, instead of a baseball mitt, Fish carried a big stack of papers. Mr. Fishman's arms were filled with books.

"More homework," said Mom. She took the papers from Fish and said, "Thank you so much for bringing these to Danny, Stephen."

Fish looked up the stairs; Mom nodded.

"Where do you want these, Gwen?" asked Mr. Fishman.

Mom pointed toward the dining room table. "This is so thoughtful of you and Stephen, Mark. I know Danny will appreciate it."

Mr. Fishman smiled. "Appreciate homework? I doubt it!"

"Coffee?"

"That would be nice," said Mr. Fishman.

Danny sat at the desk in his bedroom, a large sketch-pad in front of him, a green pencil in his hand.

"Whatcha drawing?" asked Fish.

Danny closed the cover of the sketchpad and tucked the pencil in his pocket.

"Aw, man," said Fish. "Don't do that. I like your drawings."

Fish reached for the notepad. Danny slapped his hand down on top of it.

"You know all I can draw is a stickman," said Fish. "Let me see what a real artist can do."

Fish locked eyes with Danny. Finally, Danny moved his hand away.

"I like your drawings," Fish said again. "Especially those cars. That last Lamborghini was sweet!" Suddenly Fish whistled. "Wow! A tiger!"

Fish turned the page.

"Another tiger." Fish sounded surprised. "Nice teeth. I mean, not nice teeth. Scary teeth. And another tiger, running. Tigers, man. I never knew you liked tigers so much."

Danny shook his head; Fish understood.

"So you don't like tigers. Well, who does? Especially ones with teeth like that!" Fish pointed to the unfinished drawing Danny had just been working on. The front fangs were enormous and the tiger's lips were drawn back in a fierce snarl.

"Where do you get these ideas, dude?" Fish traced one of the fangs with his fingertip. "These are pretty…scary."

Danny grabbed the sketchpad back from Fish and slammed it shut.

"Hey, Yook, scary can be a good thing," said Fish. "It's probably tough to draw scary."

Danny and Fish exchanged a long look. Then Danny opened the pad to a blank page and wrote the words: "I dream about it."

Fish watched the words form on the page. He took the pencil from Danny and wrote underneath Danny's words: "The tiger?"

Danny shook his head.

"Oh, yeah," said Fish, blushing. "I can talk." He asked aloud this time. "You mean you dream about the tiger?"

Danny wrote: "Every night."

"No wonder you're so good at drawing the stripes," said Fish.

Danny lowered his head and lifted his pencil.

He wrote: "When I dream, I can scream."

Fish grinned. "A real sound? You make a real sound?"

Danny nodded.

Fish grabbed Danny's shoulder. "That's great, man!" he said. "That means you *can* talk. Maybe you just don't *want* to talk."

Danny looked sad.

Fish closed the sketchpad and pushed it back across the desk to Danny. "A lot of people who can talk don't make much sense, anyway," said Fish. Then, his face brightened. "Besides, I like you silent, Yook. This way, I can get a word in edgewise."

Danny smiled and shook his head.

"Let's go throw the ball around," said Fish, giving Danny a high five.

Dr. Rogers liked to lean back in his chair while Danny sat on the sofa.

When Dr. Rogers asked questions, sometimes Danny shrugged.

Sometimes he shook his head "no."

Sometimes he ignored Dr. Rogers and just looked out the window.

Occasionally, Danny would write down an answer.

Dr. Rogers seemed like a nice man. Danny just didn't want to think about some of the questions Dr. Rogers asked.

"I'm going to talk about the tiger for a minute, Danny," said Dr. Rogers. "Is that okay with you?"

Danny looked at his shoes. Dr. Rogers was probably going to sit there, silently, for the rest of the visit unless Danny said something. Dr. Rogers was pretty excellent at just sitting silently. He would do great in Mr. Moore's math class. So Danny nodded. Just a little nod.

"Good." Dr. Rogers twirled his pen. He did that a lot. One thing Danny had noticed over the last six months since Dad died is that, if you don't talk to people, you really notice the little things they do all the time. Shawn jiggled his knee. RJ tugged on her hair. Mom rubbed her forehead, right between her eyebrows. And Dr. Rogers twirled his pen from finger to finger, like a baton in a marching band. Maybe Dr. Rogers had been a band-leader or whatever they were called back in the day when Dr. Rogers was in high school. Danny took a close look at Dr. Rogers. His hair was getting gray around his ears. High school was probably a long time ago for good ole Dr. Rogers.

"A tiger is an interesting thing to dream about," said Dr. Rogers. "It's clear that it frightens you. And it showed up right after your father died, right, Danny?"

Dr. Rogers looked directly at Danny. Danny knew he had to nod or they'd be sitting there in dead silence again. So Danny nodded. Just a little nod.

"And in your dreams, Danny, what do you do when the tiger chases you?"

Danny shrugged.

"You run?"

Danny nodded. A little nod.

Dr. Rogers sat up in his chair and stopped twirling

his pen. That made Danny sit forward on the sofa. It was probably time to go. Mom was waiting in the lobby.

"I have an idea for you, Danny," said Dr. Rogers. "I want you to try something. Would you?"

Danny shrugged again.

"Tonight just before you fall asleep, think about this. Think about building yourself a strong, safe fortress in your dream. Build it with thick walls, and a tall tower. Build it fast, and go inside, and close the door and lock the gates."

Danny's eyes grew wide. He had never thought of that. When he dreamt about the tiger, he just ran. And ran and ran and ran until he screamed and woke himself up screaming and Mom burst into his room and held him while he screamed and sometimes even cried. A fortress. Build a fortress.

"Build it strong, Danny," said Dr. Rogers. "And let's see what that tiger does when he's faced with that."

"Shhhh!" The lady sitting in the row in front of them turned back to watch the show.

Shawn tried to hold the bag of popcorn quietly, but every time he reached into it for a handful, the bag crinkled and popped and crackled.

RJ tilted her box of SnoCaps in Danny's direction. He held his hand out, and she poured a few chocolate candies into his palm. They made a sliding sound, and the lady got up and moved over a half dozen seats.

"Way to clear the sightlines," said Shawn. RJ poked him in the arm. "Ow!" Shawn grabbed his arm and pretended he was mortally injured.

"SHHHH!" the lady hissed from the far end of the row.

Danny rolled his eyes. Shawn rolled his eyes. RJ rolled her eyes.

The speakers in the movie theater suddenly roared. On the screen, three cars and a giant truck raced down a city street, horns blaring, tired screeching.

"Shhh!" said Shawn to the screen.

RJ laughed. And Danny smiled. He hadn't smiled in a long time.

That night, Danny drew a picture before he fell asleep.

He turned to a fresh page in the sketchpad and sharpened his pencil.

He drew an enormous fortress, a huge castle with windows and flags and stairways. He drew bars over the windows and big, heavy-looking locks on the doors and gates. He drew a moat all around the fortress, filled with deep, cold water and gigantic alligators that would eat any trespassers. He drew spikes on the banks of the moat to trap invaders, and rows of soldiers along the tops of walls, ready to fight off armies. And then, in the far corner of the page, he drew a tiger. But it was small, tiny, and without teeth. That would be his dream tonight. He would surprise that tiger!

Danny fell asleep with his sketchpad still in one hand, ready to dream about building a safe place where no tigers could chase him.

He woke up screaming.

Mom rushed in, like she did each night. She was starting to look pretty tired and worried. She held Danny, like she did each night, until he stopped screaming and starting crying, softly. She kissed the top of his head and rocked him back and forth, like he was a baby, but he didn't mind. She cried a little, too. Danny could hear it in her breathing. She was probably making his hair wet. I'm sorry, Mom, thought Danny. I'm sorry I'm waking you up. I'm sorry you don't get to sleep. I'm sorry I make you sad every night.

The next morning, it was decided.

"The brown suitcase is clothes, shoes, and lots of clean underwear and socks," said Mom. "The blue suitcase has two hats, your sketchpad and pencils, and homework."

Danny made a face.

"You keep up with that homework, son," she said, sternly.

Danny nodded.

"And this bag and little cooler are food for the road for you and Uncle Bucky."

Danny raised one eyebrow.

Mom smiled. "Chocolate chip cookies. Turkey sandwiches. Cold chicken. Apples, bananas, and a big bag of carrot sticks."

Danny did not want to go. He hadn't visited Gramps in years. Maybe Gramps didn't like children. Maybe Gramps cooked weird food. Maybe Gramps didn't cook at all and they'd be eating nothing but cold cereal and crawfish. Danny had heard that people in Mississippi ate crawfish. Even though Danny had no idea of what a crawfish was, he thought that eating them sounded gross. He would not let Gramps force him to eat crawfish. Mom rubbed the top of his head. "*Lots* of chocolate chip cookies. Does that help?"

Danny nodded.

"I'll miss you, little man."

Danny cocked his head. Mom smiled again.

"OK, I'll miss you—*medium-sized* man."

Mom opened her arms. Danny held on to her tight.

# chapter SEVEN

"**W**ake up, Danny!" said Uncle Bucky, gently jostling Danny's shoulder. "We're almost there."

Danny blinked his eyes and sat up to stretch. He hoped he had not yelled about the tiger while he slept in the car. Danny checked Uncle Bucky's face; he didn't look worried, and he didn't mention anything about tigers. Good. Maybe tigers don't visit dreams during daytime naps, thought Danny.

"Hey, sleepyhead," said Uncle Bucky. "Grab me one of your mother's cookies, would you?"

Danny dug his into in the bag and emerged with a big cookie in his hand. Uncle Bucky snatched it and took a bite. Danny dug out another cookie and nibbled on it as he rested his head on the window and saw what Mississippi looked like. Wide, pretty streets. Low houses and big, white buildings with tall columns. Church steeples. Green gardens. Old trees. Lots of pickup trucks.

"Spring in Mississippi," said Uncle Bucky. "Magnolias will be in bloom soon. Lovely things, magnolias."

Danny nodded, though he wasn't exactly certain what a magnolia would be. But just about anything in bloom was a pretty thing, he figured.

Danny had not been to Gramps's house in a long, long while. Since he was too little to remember. Since he was in a car seat.

It was a nine-hour drive almost straight south to the little Mississippi town where Gramps lived. Danny had a vague memory of a long, one-story house with a big front porch in a row of other long houses with similar porches. He didn't know if that was a real memory or just from a picture his mom had on the refrigerator.

Uncle Bucky parked his car behind the house.

"If I know your Gramps, he'll be sitting out on the porch, rockin' and talkin'," said Bucky.

Rockin' and talkin', thought Danny. He liked how those words fit together. Mom would say, "Just like your father."

And now Danny was here, just outside the house where his daddy had grown up.

Without Daddy.

The garden behind Gramps's house had a few scraggly tomato plants in it.

It didn't look like Gramps was much of a gardener. Those plants looked thirsty to Danny.

Next to the tomatoes, there was a small shed. It needed paint. It had a hole for a window, but the glass had fallen out long ago.

Uncle Bucky led the way up three cement steps to the back door.

Before the screen door had a chance to creak, Gramps bellowed out to them from the front porch.

"Son!"

Danny jumped a foot. Man! Gramps had a *loud* voice. Dad had been right. If Gramps was that loud on the front porch, all the neighbors knew Uncle Bucky had just gotten home.

"Son, you know where I am!" yelled Gramps. "Bring the boy here!"

Danny wondered if Twigs, a famous bellower himself, would grow up to be as loud and bossy as Gramps. Maybe. Maybe not.

There was no hallway to the house, just one room opening into the next. Uncle Bucky led the way through the sparkling clean kitchen with a bathroom off in one corner, a dining room with a sofa bed along one wall, a bedroom with two beds and a television, and then a living room.

A lot of books, thought Danny.

"Dad likes a lot of books," said Uncle Bucky.

Through the window at the front of the house, Danny could see the outline of Gramps sitting in a rocking chair on the porch. The front door was standing open. Gramps did not turn around. "Grandson! Come here, young man!"

Danny thought that Gramps's big voice made the door rattle in its frame. But maybe that was just Danny's imagination.

Uncle Bucky smiled and held open the front door.

Gramps's front porch was like another room inside the house. A long brown sofa hugged the outside house wall and faced the street. A table with four chairs held leftovers from lunch and a pitcher half-filled with iced tea. A creaky rocker squeaked as Gramps sipped tea and stared over the top of his glass at Danny.

Gramps cocked his head toward another rocking chair, slightly smaller than his own.

"Take a seat!" said Gramps.

Danny headed for the chair.

"Pour yourself some tea, first!" Gramps was so loud that everything he said sounded like an order he was shouting.

Danny stopped at the table. It held ice in a bucket, two unused glasses on a tray, a white crockery bowl filled with lemon wedges, and a bowl of leaves. Danny had no idea if he even liked iced tea, much less iced tea with leaves in it.

Gramps noticed Danny hesitating. "That's sweet tea!" barked Gramps. "Sugar's in the tea, already. I make it that way."

But why are there leaves? Danny wanted to ask. He picked up the bowl of greens, turned around to Gramps, and raised his other hand, palm up.

"Mint!" said Gramps. "I grow it myself! Stick a leaf in your tea! See what you think!"

Danny scooped ice cubes into one glass. He carefully lifted the heavy glass pitcher and poured.

"Your Uncle Bucky takes his with extra mint!" ordered Gramps.

Danny grabbed the second glass and repeated the process. He picked one green leaf out of the bowl and dropped it into his glass. Was one too much? Too little? How much would Uncle Bucky's "extra mint" be, Danny wondered?

"Three leaves, bud," said Uncle Bucky, walking out onto the porch and closing the screen door quietly behind him. There he goes again, magically reading my mind, thought Danny. How *does* he do that?

Uncle Bucky took the end of the sofa nearest Gramps. He accepted the glass from Danny with a nod.

Danny took the rocker.

The three men sipped their tea. Two of them rocked slowly.

Danny liked the quiet that happened when Gramps was not shouting.

They all stared out at the empty street, where absolutely nothing was happening.

But eventually, Gramps spoke. He wasn't *quite* shouting this time, but Danny was sure the people living in the house across the street could still hear.

"In the morning, I make breakfast," said Gramps. "You wash the dishes. Then, we talk."

In the room with two beds, Danny's suitcases were sitting by the bed nearest the television.

To get to the bathroom or the kitchen during the night, he'd have to walk through the dining room with the sofa bed. How would he not wake up Gramps?

"Gramps is used to me walking through his room," said Uncle Bucky.

Danny jumped and eyed Uncle Bucky suspiciously. Uncle Bucky shrugged.

"He's gotta walk through ours to get to the porch. And he is one early riser." Uncle Bucky chuckled to himself.

Danny unzipped the brown suitcase. Under neatly folded underwear and tee shirts, he found a pair of flannel pajamas.

"Just the bottoms," said Uncle Bucky. "Mississippi. Hot nights."

Danny set the top back into the suitcase.

"I'll go brush my teeth first," said Uncle Bucky. "Then you can have the bathroom." Uncle Bucky left the room, and Danny sat down on the edge of his bed and looked around.

Uncle Bucky said Gramps liked books, but Uncle Bucky seemed to read a lot, too. Short stacks of books were lined up in even piles under Uncle Bucky's bed. Books on art and drawing on the left. Books on the Mississippi River and New Orleans in the middle. On the right, books with titles that didn't tell you what they were about, written by Faulkner, Dickey, Baldwin, and Irving.

Next to Uncle Bucky's bed, a table held a glass jar of pencils, a spiral-bound sketchpad, and a black Baltimore Ravens hat with a big, purple raven on the front. There were also two framed photographs, which Danny had to walk over to in order to see. One was old: Gramps standing in front of this house holding one boy in his left arm and holding the hand of an older boy, who was standing on his right. The other one Danny knew well; Mom had a copy, too. She took it on Danny's last birthday, before Dad had been deployed again. It had been their anniversary. Mom had made pot roast, Dad's favorite dinner. Dad had given Mom a present, a new phone, all charged and ready to go. Mom couldn't figure out how to take a picture with it, and was laughing at herself. Dad and Danny were laughing, too. Dad put his arm around Danny's shoulders, pointed at Mom, and click! She accidentally took a really good picture. "My two men," she had said then. Now she just had one man. Me, thought Danny. And I'm not much of a man, really.

Danny leaned over Uncle Bucky's neatly made bed to see the three framed drawings hanging on the wall. They were done in pencil, so you had to get in good and close to see the details. That's what Dad used to say, anyway: "Don't be shy. Get in good and close. Study the details. The artist put them there for you to find."

One wasn't really a drawing of a scene or a thing, but was a map of the state of Mississippi. The pencil work was intricate and detailed, with town names carefully lettered: Vicksburg, Jackson, Hattiesburg, and others. The west border of the state was the Mississippi River, and the river was as twisted as a piece of curling ribbon on a Christmas package, thought Danny. Lakes and train tracks were drawn in, but not highways, and tucked underneath the southern edge of the state, next door in Louisiana, was New Orleans. The way the letters were drawn made it clear that the artist really liked New Orleans.

"I always liked New Orleans," said Uncle Bucky, walking back into the room.

Danny pointed to the drawing hanging next to the map.

"I did that back in high school," said Uncle Bucky. "That's Gramps, out back, doing his barbecue." In the drawing, Gramps was younger, a little skinnier, standing straight and tall with a long pair of tongs in one hand. His grin nearly stretched ear and to ear, and Danny found himself grinning back at the drawing as if Gramps could see him.

"And you know who this is." Uncle Bucky pointed to the third framed drawing on the wall. Dad, holding a fat baby under the arms, forehead-to-forehead.

I was fat, thought Danny. Uncle Bucky laughed. "You were one fat baby!"

"My big brother," said Uncle Bucky. "And my nephew." He drew in a shaky breath, and his eyes moistened.

He lost his brother, thought Danny. I lost my dad, but Uncle Bucky lost his brother. Suddenly, Danny felt like he could cry and cry and cry.

Uncle Bucky's hand brushed Danny's arm. "You go brush your teeth, now. Get ready for bed."

Danny had meant to write a note to Uncle Bucky before bedtime, apologizing in case he woke up screaming. But when he got back to the room after brushing his teeth, the light was off and Uncle Bucky was in bed.

I'd probably scare Uncle Bucky half to death if I yell at night, Danny thought.

And then: What do I mean, "if"? Every night, I dream about the tiger, and every night, I wake up screaming. It will happen. And I will wake him up. And probably Gramps, too. Like a little baby, screaming in the night.

Danny rolled over and faced the wall. He took a deep breath and blew it out slowly. Don't dream about the tiger, he thought. Don't. Don't do it.

"I wake up most every night from Gramps's snoring. I can hear it right through that wall," said Uncle Bucky.

"So if you need to yell at that tiger you dream about, you go right ahead. You can't scare me."

That Uncle Bucky, thought Danny. He was one scary mind reader.

# chapter EIGHT

From inside his fortress, Danny could see the tiger prowling the grounds beyond the moat.

It had grown even bigger. The muscles of its forelegs bunched powerfully as it moved. It never took its eyes off him. Danny ducked down behind the fortress wall and peeked through a chink between the stones. The tiger's eyes found him and locked.

It sees me, thought Danny. It still sees me.

At the narrowest point of the moat, the tiger stopped moving. It backed up one step, then two.

It's going to jump the moat, thought Danny. It's coming for me.

The tiger half-squatted, its powerful haunches preparing for the leap.

It opened its mouth and roared.

The roar was so loud and so long that Danny felt the tiger's breath on his face, felt the rage in that roar, felt the anger in the air that blew past him. Danny rocked back on his heels.

And bumped into something. Danny felt the scream bubbling up in his throat.

"I'm right here, bud," said a voice behind him. "I'm right here."

Terrified, Danny whirled around to face the danger. And was suddenly happier than he had been in months.

"Dad!"

Maple syrup would taste great on these pancakes, Danny thought, but he couldn't make enough sound to ask for it.

He'd like another glass of orange juice, but he couldn't make himself say "please," and he knew Gramps would expect good manners.

Uncle Bucky passed him the syrup, poured him more orange juice, and said, "We know you can say at least one word."

Danny raised one eyebrow.

"Last night," said Uncle Bucky. "Last night you yelled 'Dad!'"

Gramps grunted and rustled the newspaper he was reading. Gramps didn't seem to make much sound in the morning.

Danny poured the syrup over three more pancakes.

"You have an appetite, I'll give you that," said Uncle Bucky.

Danny remembered. He had seen Dad in his dream last night! And Dad had felt as real as Gramps and Uncle Bucky felt today! Danny couldn't even remember whether or not the tiger had jumped; all he could remember was that he had hugged Dad harder than any hug they had ever had when Dad was still here.

And then suddenly Danny wasn't hungry at all and his cheeks were wet and he set down his fork and ran to his bedroom.

Uncle Bucky rose up out of his chair.

"Stay, son," said Gramps quietly. "We all need to find our way."

"This is my favorite path through the woods," said Gramps, pointing to the right fork in a worn path between two birches. "And this—" he pointed to the left fork "—is the path to Miss Sally's store, should you ever find need of a candy bar or a comic book. Your daddy walked *that* path many a day. Your Uncle Bucky, too."

Where's that third path go? thought Danny. He tugged on Gramps's shirtsleeve and pointed.

"Ah, there," said Gramps. "Well, you won't be needing that path. At least, anytime soon."

Out here in the woods, Gramps's voice didn't seem that loud. Maybe the trees and the flowers sucked up the sound, thought Danny. He kept his steps slow, so that he wouldn't get ahead of Gramps.

With his cane, Gramps poked a green plant alongside the path. "That's a jack-in-the-pulpit, right there." Danny looked at it, just to be polite. He really didn't care much about plants. "Lift that top leaf there, grandson."

Danny grabbed the end of the leaf and pulled it up. Red berries, like little jewels.

"Huh!" said Gramps. "Imagine that!"

Danny dropped the leaf back into place, hiding the berries.

"There's a clearing up ahead. We might see some wild hyacinth starting to bud. You come back in a few weeks, and that whole meadow will be purple with bloom."

Danny didn't want to be here in a few weeks. He was happy to be visiting Gramps and Uncle Bucky, and Gramps made delicious pancakes, but if Danny stayed here that long, he would miss RJ. He would miss Shawn. He would miss Twigs. He'd like to see Twigs and Gramps in a shouting match! He would miss Fish. And Mom.

Up ahead, Danny saw a tower of red. A huge plant with huge flowers. Monster-sized flowers, like dinner plates! The blooms looked like Christmas poinsettias, each one a five-leafed giant star. The plant was taller than Danny. He pointed, and then turned to face Gramps.

"Ah, that's a treasure, now," said Gramps. "Swamp hibiscus. It likes to keep its feet wet, so I don't often find one along this path—though it is on the damp side of the woods." Gramps stopped and smiled at the flower. "Isn't that a pretty thing? Some people hate these—they aren't subtle! But they always make me smile."

They walked a bit further along the path, content to be in each other's company, content to be quiet. Danny thought he could get used to Gramps's shouting when he talked, as long as there were lots of nice times like this one, times when they were quiet together.

"Here's why it's my favorite path," said Gramps. The path veered out of the woods and into a clearing. "That's the wild hyacinth I told you about." Gramps pointed with his cane. The clearing sloped down to a small creek. It was shallow, running fast, and making a bubbling, rushing sound. As they stood there, a small deer stepped delicately out of the brush and crossed to the creek. It lowered its head to the water.

"An older fawn," said Gramps. He was being pretty quiet—for Gramps. "See the fading spots?"

Danny had never seen such a young deer.

"I suppose its mother is around here somewhere," said Gramps. And she stepped out the woods, too, on slender, elegant legs, to sip at the brook beside her baby.

"Another pretty thing," said Gramps.

At its mother's arrival, the fawn lifted its head and nuzzled at its mother's flank.

"See, now, it's too old to nurse, but it still remembers," said Gramps. "Mama is comfort." They watched the fawn and doe until Gramps cleared his throat. Danny looked up at Gramps's face, a little whiskery and a lot wrinkly, and saw that Gramps's eyes were brimming.

Gramps, are you okay? Danny wanted to ask. But his voice would not come. He lost his son, Danny thought. I lost my dad, and Gramps lost his son.

Danny couldn't say what he wanted to say. Then he thought, even if I could speak, I'm not sure I would know what to say. I miss him, too? How would that help? How would anything help? Dad was gone, and never coming home again, and it was stupid, and no one could fix that, not even Gramps. Thinking like that make Danny's stomach hurt, and a tight, angry ball in his chest burned and burned.

But Danny wasn't mad at Gramps. And Gramps probably felt mad, just like Danny, some days. And since Danny could not make a sound to help, as he and his grandfather watched the fawn and the doe stand close together in the little meadow clearing by the brook,

Danny shifted his weight and leaned against Gramps arm. I'm here, Gramps, he thought. I'm not him, but I'm here.

After Danny and Gramps returned home from their walk, Gramps had pressed a few dollar bills into Danny's hand and pointed out the way to Miss Sally's.

"You go on, now," said Gramps. "Go do what boys do."

So Danny had followed the left fork of the woodlands path. It rose over a small hill and curved down into a meadow that edged the backdoors and back gardens of the far edge of the outskirts of town. At the end of the path, before the rows of small cottages began, sat three little buildings: a café, a gas station, and a shop with no sign or awning, but with "Miss Sally's" painted over the door in curly yellow letters.

The door opened with the sound of a tinkling bell.

It was dim inside. So dim that it was hard for Danny to see. But he could smell.

Miss Sally's store smelled like fresh bread and fried chicken and chocolate and paper: books and magazines and comic books. Danny's eyes got used to the light. Now he could see.

A menu on the wall: chicken and ribs and biscuits. A long counter with an ancient-looking cash register and an even more ancient-looking little old lady. Shelves of canned goods and boxes of things like stuffing and instant mashed potatoes. An open cooler filled with vegetables and fruit. And against the back wall, a rack of—yes!—comic books!

But there was a catch.

Two boys and a girl stood by the comic books, laughing and reading.

Danny wanted to see the latest issue of *Superior Spider-Man*, and maybe *Adventure Time*, too, if Miss Sally had it. He waited a few minutes by the vegetables, trying to act like he was actually interested in green beans, but those kids didn't look like they were going to move. Finally, he walked over to the comic book display.

He caught the eye of the tallest boy and nodded. Then Danny focused on the comic books. Yes! *Adventure Time!* But if he reached for the issue, he'd have to ask the shorter boy to move. And how could he ask?

The high, reedy voice of Miss Sally carried over from her post beside the cash register. "Michael and Aaron, that's Mr. Yukon's grandson, Danny, standing there! Your mothers raised you to have good manners—you show some, now."

"Hey," said the tall one. "I'm Michael." He put out his hand, and Danny shook it.

"Aaron," said the short one, also offering his hand. But he didn't smile.

"And introduce him to your pretty lady friend, too," said Miss Sally.

"I'm Lily," said the girl. "Pleased to meet you."

Danny nodded to each of them. He opened his mouth as if he would speak, but that was silly. Of course, no sound would come out. He didn't want them to think that he was so stuck up he wouldn't speak to them. He wondered how to make them understand. So instead, he tried to reach behind Aaron to get the issue of *Adventure Time*.

Aaron glared at Danny and did not budge.

Danny reached around Aaron, bumped into him, but managed to grab the comic book.

"Hey!" yelled Aaron. "Knock it off!"

Danny lifted the comic book to show Aaron, but Aaron didn't understand.

"Say 'excuse me,' or something," said Aaron. "Rude, dude."

Danny shook his head no. He raised his hand higher to show Aaron the comic book again. Aaron thought Danny raised his hands to fight. Aaron gave Danny a hard shove, and Danny staggered back. He couldn't even make a sound when he was surprised and hurt.

"Aaron!" Lily looked angry.

Michael stepped up and for a moment, Danny thought Michael was going to hit him, too. But Michael put a flat hand on Aaron's chest, instead.

"Dumb move, Aaron," said Michael.

Tiny Miss Sally suddenly appeared behind Danny. How did she move so fast? And so silently? She had sparkling blue eyes and a face as wrinkled as a dried apple. She was so short that Danny could see she held her white hair up in a bun with dozens of little silver bobby pins.

"Mornin', Miss Sally," said Michael, Aaron, and Lily.

"Mornin' to you, young people," she said. And just stood there. Michael dropped his hand from Aaron's chest and stepped back. Aaron lowered his fists. Danny was grateful.

"And I'm pleased to meet you, Mr. Yukon." Miss Sally smiled at Danny. "Your grandfather has been telling me all about you since the day you were born."

There was an awkward silence. Danny should have replied to Miss Sally, but could not speak. Aaron's face was red, and he looked angry with Michael for pushing him. When Aaron looked at Danny, his face got even redder.

"As you can tell," said Lily, in a slow drawl that made her sound to Danny like a character in a movie, "Miss Sally knows everything about everybody in this town."

Michael spoke. "Miss Sally, I'd like this *Spider-Man*, please." He handed her the comic book he had been holding.

"I want licorice," said Aaron, and stomped off to the candy aisle.

"My momma sent me with a list," said Lily. She smiled at Danny. "I'd better start shopping."

Miss Sally and Danny were left alone, standing by the comic books. Thank you, Danny thought, and nodded his head at her. She raised one eyebrow and pointed to a sign lettered in pink magic marker, hanging over the comic book stand: "You read it, you buy it!!!"

Danny followed Miss Sally's glance down to his right hand and the issue of *Adventure Time*. Oh! He thought. He reached into his jeans pocket and pulled out the folded bills from Gramps.

"I'll see *you* at the cash register, Mr. Yukon," said Miss Sally.

Uncle Bucky sat on the front porch, looking down at his feet. An untouched glass of iced tea sat on the table near him.

The front door was ajar.

When Danny's foot hit the bottom step, Uncle Bucky's head came up.

Uncle Bucky's eyes looked as sad as any eyes Danny had even seen. Had something bad happened? Mom? Was Mom hurt? How about Gramps? Was Gramps okay?

Uncle Bucky shook his head. "No new troubles, young man. No new troubles."

That made Danny feel a little relieved, but Uncle Bucky still looked so sad. Danny sat down in the smaller rocker and waited.

After a short while, Uncle Bucky put his hand on Danny's shoulder. "No new troubles, young man. Just visiting some familiar ones." Uncle Bucky pushed his chair back from the table, and the wooden legs scraped the painted porch floor. "Mailman came by and brought some familiar troubles."

Uncle Bucky stood and walked into the house.

Familiar troubles, thought Danny. Dad.

Gramps stood in the bedroom Danny shared with Uncle Bucky, staring at the wall of Uncle Bucky's drawings as if he had never seen them before. Gramps's eyes were wet, and in his hands he held a folded piece of paper.

Danny wanted to ask Gramps what was wrong. Instead, he stood next to Gramps and looked at the wall, just as Gramps was doing. The map of Mississippi with the detail of New Orleans. Gramps as a younger man, barbecue tongs in hand, grinning and happy. And Dad, holding the baby Danny. Uncle Bucky was a good artist, thought Danny. But Dad was, perhaps, a little bit better. Dad *had been* better, Danny corrected himself.

A rustle of paper unfolding.

"Came in this morning's mail," said Gramps. He coughed once. "They sent his belongings home to your mama, and she sent this on to us."

Danny looked down at Gramps's hands at a creased piece of rough newsprint. The drawing Dad had shown him when they Skyped from Afghanistan, long months ago. Close up, the drawing looked even more lifelike: Danny and Gramps, their heads close together and bent down a bit, both of them concentrating.

"Tying your shoe," said Gramps.

What? Danny thought.

"I was teaching you how to tie your shoe there," said Gramps. "You were, oh, I suppose about 4 years old. You don't see the shoe in the drawing, but I remember the picture. Your dad must have carried that picture with him over there."

Why are we staring at the wall? thought Danny. He wasn't sure, but he stood there, next to Gramps. The paper rustled a little more. Gramps's hands were shaky.

Gramps cleared his throat with a gravelly cough. "Tape's in the top drawer there," he announced.

Danny was puzzled.

"Tape's in the drawer!" Gramps boomed.

Yes sir! Gramps sure liked to give orders, Danny thought grumpily. He handed Gramps the roll of tape.

Gramps wide big, long fingers. Danny figured Gramps would never be able to text on a cell phone or even dial a friend without hitting all the wrong numbers. Tie a shoe? How on earth could he have done that? Yet he must have, somehow, because I know how to tie my shoes, Danny thought.

Carefully, slowly, Gramps attached a tiny strip of tape to each corner of the drawing. "Gonna frame this later," he said aloud, but Danny wasn't sure Gramps was really talking to him.

And then Gramps walked to the wall over Uncle Bucky's bed.

"Here?" he asked Danny, holding the new drawing near the map of Mississippi. Danny didn't like it there. He thought the new drawing of him and Gramps should go next to the drawing of him and Dad. Sort of like him growing up, right there on the wall.

A slam of the front screen door. Footsteps into the room.

"No," said Uncle Bucky, still looking sad. He pointed. "Put it up there, next to David. And Danny."

# chapter NINE

Once Danny had dreamed about seeing his father, Gramps never had to say "Bedtime" or even point at the clock. Danny was eager to go to bed. Maybe he would dream about Dad again!

For a night or two, he didn't. But then he did.

Danny dreamt that he was walking on a path through the woods. Suddenly, the single path split into two paths. And then into three. And then into six. Which way should he go?

He could hear a sound off to the right, a sound of something cheerful. He picked the path headed that way, and started to walk.

It led straight out of the woods into a wide clearing. In the center of the meadow stood a messy pile of stones. As Danny got closer, he could see the stones were from his fortress. The tower had collapsed. The walls were broken down. Gray and black stones lay all over the grassy ground.

The cheerful sound was a man whistling a happy song. The whistling was coming from behind a tall pile of stones.

Danny walked around the pile

"Dad!" he yelled.

Dad smiled and held up one finger. "Shhh!" he said. "You'll wake your uncle."

"Dad," Danny whispered. "Dad, I am so glad to see you!"

Dad's smile was the biggest one Danny had ever seen him wear. "I'm glad to see you, too, son."

Dad was holding a stone in one hand and a trowel in the other. He dipped the trowel into a pan of mortar, scraped off the extra on the edge of the pan, and then spread the mortar along one side of the stone. Then Dad carefully set the stone on top of a wall of similar stones.

"How did this fall down?" asked Danny.

"This is a fine fortress, son," said Dad. "This wall is worth rebuilding."

"But how did it fall?" asked Danny, again.

"I'm not sure," said Dad. "But maybe you didn't think you could build a strong fortress all by yourself."

So Danny and Dad worked side-by-side, building the wall. They worked and worked on it, until the wall reached high into the sky. They did not have ladders, so Danny did not understand how they could build a wall that kept growing, but that was the way of dreams.

Things just happened in dreams, whether you understood them or not.

It was a hot, hot afternoon. Afternoons were often hot in Mississippi. It was so hot that Gramps wasn't sitting on the front porch. He was sitting on the sofa in the living room, reading a book in the bright light from the window.

Danny turned the last page of *Adventure Time* and wondered if Miss Sally would have the next issue in her store yet. He set the comic book aside and stood up to stretch.

Gramps raised one eyebrow but did not lift his eyes from the page he was reading.

Danny walked through the bedroom he shared with Uncle Bucky. He walked through Gramps's bedroom. He walked into the kitchen and looked out the back window.

Man, those tomato plants looked sad.

Danny took a glass from the counter, filled it at the sink with cold water, and walked out the back door.

At the sound of the screen door banging shut, Gramps looked up.

Then Gramps stood up and stretched, too. He walked through the bedroom Danny shared with Uncle Bucky, and then through his own bedroom. Gramps walked into the kitchen and looked out the back window.

He saw Danny walk over to the three scrawny tomato plants Gramps had almost forgotten he had planted. Danny bent over and crouched down low. Then he gave each plant a drink of water out of a plastic kitchen glass.

That made Gramps smile.

Aaron stood on the sidewalk, holding up his red-and-silver bicycle. He looked up from the sidewalk to Danny, who was rocking on the porch.

Aaron asked again. "So. Did your dead dad give you a bike?"

Michael socked Aaron in the arm, and, to Danny, it looked like it was the kind of punch that might have actually hurt a little.

"What?!" yelled Aaron, rubbing his shoulder and glaring at Michael. "I was just asking! It's not my fault the little creep can't talk!"

Michael tried to change the subject. "You wanna ride bikes with us, man?"

Danny didn't know whether Gramps had a bike or not, so Danny just shook his head no.

Michael nodded, and for a moment, gave Danny a look that seemed to be kind.

Michael and Aaron rode off on their bikes.

Danny stopped rocking. He sat and thought. And then he thought some more.

From inside the house, Gramps looked out the living room window onto the porch, and thought, too.

That night, Danny dreamt about the path again.

Again, the single path split into many paths. The cheerful whistling began, and Danny followed it to the meadow.

There was Dad! Three walls of the fortress stood now, fine and strong.

"These walls are fine and strong," said Dad, whistling as he kept working. They could both hear the tiger growling and prowling off in the forest.

"Funny," said Danny. "That was just what I was thinking!"

Dad laughed at that, long and hard. He put one arm around Danny's shoulders and gave him a squeeze. "Father and son," he said. "Father and son."

Something about that made Danny feel a little sad and a little happy at the same time.

"Well!" said Dad. "What do you say? Should we get to work and finish building this fortress of yours? That tiger is still out there. You have to be ready."

Now Danny felt sad without feeling happy at all. "But—" said Danny.

His father stopped whistling and looked up. "Yes, son?"

"But if we finish building it, won't you have to leave?"

When Danny woke up, there were tears on his cheeks.

The back screen door kept banging.

Every now and then, Gramps made a funny sound. An "uuumph!" or a "grrrrr!" or a grunt. Then the screen door would bang again.

Clop clop clop. Gramps shoes made a big noise when they hit the back steps.

Danny pulled the pillow over his head but it didn't keep out the noise.

Uncle Bucky set up his computer at the kitchen table to Skype with Mom.

Danny had a lemonade. Uncle Bucky had iced tea with mint. A plate of ginger cookies from Miss Sally's sat on the table next to the laptop.

Gramps came in from the back yard when the call went through.

Mom's face appeared, and she smiled a sad smile when she saw Danny's on her own screen. "There you are!" she said, and touched the screen. Like she used to do with Dad, Danny thought.

"How are you, honey?" Mom's voice sounded funny and tight. Danny knew she was really asking: "Can you speak yet?" He felt sad that he could not shout, "Yes!" and make her smile happier.

"Your son is doing just fine, Gwen!" Gramps yelled.

Mom smiled. "I can hear you, Daniel. No need to yell."

"He *is* doing fine, Gwen," said Uncle Bucky. "He doesn't miss you at all." He elbowed Danny, who pulled away and elbowed Uncle Bucky back.

"Are these two telling me the truth, little man?" asked Mom. "You doing all right?"

Danny nodded. He held up new comic book.

"Ah!" said Mom. "The latest copy?"

Danny nodded again.

"Now, don't you just sit inside reading," said Mom. "You take yourself out and do something."

Danny wished he could tell her about the mother deer and the baby deer. About the paths Gramps showed him through the woods. About nice Michael and crabby Aaron and pretty Lily. About the amazingly short Miss Sally.

But he couldn't, so he just smiled at her face on the computer screen.

Then Gramps leaned in and hogged the computer camera.

"Gwen!" he shouted.

Mom laughed a soft little laugh. "I'm here, Daniel."

"Gwen," said Gramps. "Now, don't you worry."

Dinner was fried chicken from Miss Sally's, with a salad Uncle Bucky made that was full of mushrooms and onions and broccoli.

Gramps ate two pieces of chicken. Uncle Bucky ate three. Danny picked at one. Miss Sally made great chicken, but Danny didn't feel hungry.

"A little homesick for Mom?" asked Uncle Bucky.

Danny shrugged. Uncle Bucky rubbed the top of Danny's head. Uncle Bucky had big hands, like Dad's.

Gramps stood up and cleared his plate.

"Grandson," he said, turning around from the sink. "Come with me."

Danny followed Gramps out the back screen door. Uncle Bucky caught it before it banged, and held it open. He stood on the back steps, watching Gramps and Danny walk around the little garden patch.

As they passed the tomatoes, Gramps grunted. "Those look a little happier than usual," he said, without looking at Danny.

Gramps stopped at the little shed. He unlatched a hook on the door and held it open. "Go on ahead in, young man."

What could be in that little shed, thought Danny? A rake? A lawn mower? Spiders? A few mice? He wasn't so sure he wanted to go into that shed at all.

But Gramps stood there, waiting. And so Danny put one foot in front of the other, and walked to Gramps. Gramps put a hand on Danny's back, and steered him through the door.

Danny was surprised.

The shed was not full of cobwebs and dust. It was bright and clean and had whitewashed walls and a little rocking chair. The rocking chair from the porch, Danny thought. The missing window had been replaced with real glass.

A small table held a lantern and a book of fables and fairy tales. Danny touched the cover of the book.

"That was one of your father's favorites," said Gramps.

Danny lifted the book, opened it, and turned the pages. *Bluebeard. Beauty and the Beast. Aladdin and His Magic Lamp.* Each story began with a full page drawing: a bearded man with a sword in his hand, a monster standing on a castle wall next to a pretty girl, and a frightened boy staring at a genie bubbling up out of a lamp. It wasn't like a lamp you'd plug into a wall. It wasn't like the lamps Mr. Fishman packed into the back of his station wagon. It looked a little like the gravy pitcher Mom used at Thanksgiving.

Danny set the book down and looked around the rest of the shed. The walls were covered with drawings and pictures.

There was a photograph of Gramps, Uncle Bucky, Mom, and Dad sitting in the grass somewhere, laughing. Mom didn't really look like Mom because her hair was so long.

There were drawings of monsters and castles and trucks and tanks. "Your father drew those when he was not much older than you are now," said Gramps.

Photographs were taped up to the walls, too. There was a photo of Dad, looking skinny and young, in a football uniform in front of the high school. A photo of Dad and Bucky holding fishing rods and three fish strung on a line. A photo of Dad in a plaid flannel shirt, hunched over a table with a lantern on it, thinking hard and drawing a picture.

A plaid flannel shirt hung over the back on the rocking chair. Danny saw it, and looked up at Gramps. Gramps nodded. Danny reached over and touched the shirt.

Danny looked all around the little shed. Dad, Dad, Dad.

"That place where they buried your father, that's a long way from here," said Gramps. "It's a long way from where you and your mother live. Seems to me that's a long way from anywhere."

Danny looked down at his shoes and tried hard not to cry.

"I thought you might like a place you could visit your Dad, right here. Close by. A sit and think place. Your dad is not so far away here."

Danny looked up at Gramps. Danny wanted to say thank you. But he thought, even if I *could* speak, I would probably just cry anyway.

Gramps looked over at the photos on the wall. Danny swallowed hard and tried to not look too sad. Gramps held on to the back of the rocking chair and leaned toward the wall a bit. He reached out one long-fingered hand and touched the face of Dad in the picture of him in his football uniform.

"Fine boy," Gramps whispered, almost to himself. "Fine boy." Gramps set his hand on Danny's head, gave it a little rub, and then turned and walked back to the house.

Danny sat down in the little rocking chair. He looked around the shed, at the drawings and the pictures. He reached over to the little table and picked up the book of fairy tales and fables. He opened it to the story *Aladdin and His Magic Lamp.* Then he leaned his head back on the soft flannel shirt that used to be his father's and began to read.

# chapter TEN

**D**anny fell asleep in the rocking chair.

He dreamt he was walking through the woods with Gramps. They walked along the path they took the day after he came to Gramps's house. Just as they had done on that day, they stopped to look at the jack-in-the-pulpit with its hidden red berries. They stopped to admire the hibiscus with blooms like giant red stars. Then they stopped to look at the meadow where they had seen the fawn and its mother.

In the dream, the fawn stepped gracefully out of the trees. Its mother followed behind. And then the entire meadow burst into bloom with purple wild hyacinth, the flowers Gramps had told him would bloom in about a month, if he stayed in Mississippi. In Danny's dream, the air smelled like when Mom took a shower, all flowery and sweet and soft.

Danny and Gramps watched the fawn and its mother sip from the creek. The hyacinth flowers moved gently in the breeze. Then the deer turned around and returned to the woods, picking their way through the vast field of purple blooms.

Danny looked up to Gramps and wanted to say, "Isn't that beautiful?" But before Danny could speak, he and Gramps were back on the path, walking home, in that funny way that dreams work.

When they got to the fork in the path where the path to Miss Sally's began, Gramps gave Danny a little nudge.

"Now, you go on, Grandson," he said. He pointed to the third path, the one Danny thought of as the Secret Path.

"But you told me I wouldn't be needing that path soon!" said Danny. "Me? Go on that path alone?" Danny felt a little scared of that idea. Where did the Secret Path lead? How long was the Secret Path? Would there be flower and deer along the way, or would it be dark and dangerous?

Gramps nodded. "You go on, now," he said. "It's time."

Danny set one foot on the path. He turned to wave to Gramps, but suddenly, Gramps was gone and Danny was far down the path already. He walked and walked and the path seemed to keep getting longer. It felt as if he wasn't getting anywhere at all.

Then the air all around the path grew dark, and then sparkly with tiny, flying lights. The trees seemed to fall back, and only one tree was left standing in a clearing. Danny didn't know the name of the kind of tree, but it had a wide trunk and branches that seemed somehow friendly. Under the tree, right on the ground near the roots, sat a man. His eyes were closed. His knees were crossed and his feet were up by his hips—in second grade, his teacher used to call that position "Criss-cross, applesauce." His hands were open on his lap, and in them was—a lamp! A lamp like the lamp in the story about Aladdin.

Danny walked slowly around the tree in a big circle. He wanted to see the face of the man, but in his dream, the tree just kept getting taller and wider. Danny could never quite see the man's face.

"Are you a genie?" asked Danny, in his dream.

The man's voice floated out from under the tree. A familiar voice, though Danny could not think of who owned it.

"No," said the voice, kindly. "But *you* are."

Danny woke up with a jump.

A dream! A dream without the tiger in it!

That was the first one he could remember since Dad died.

Danny looked down at the book on his lap, open to the story of the magic lamp. Why had he dreamed of Aladdin?

Danny smiled. Oh, who cares? He thought. At least I dreamt a dream. It was a dream that didn't make me scream out loud. It was a dream without a tiger in it. It was a dream without tiger teeth. It was a dream without Dad.

And then Danny stopped smiling.

Uncle Bucky built a stack of five—five!—big pancakes and poured maple syrup over all of them.

Gramps just shook his head, but Danny thought he saw a little smile on Gramps's face.

Danny built a pancake stack of only three pancakes. Uncle Bucky poured maple syrup over Danny's pancakes, too.

"Fine day for a bike ride!" boomed Gramps, washing the frying pan in the sink.

Gramps rode a bike? Danny's eyebrows shot up.

"Miss Sally tells me that three young people ride their bikes to her store every morning," said Gramps. "Lily, and Michael, and some rascal named Aaron?"

Danny stopped chewing. He looked at Uncle Bucky. Then he looked at Gramps. Then he looked at Uncle Bucky again.

Uncle Bucky shrugged. "Don't blame me, little dude."

Gramps just smiled.

Uncle Bucky looked at Danny and winked. "Right after breakfast, Dad," said Uncle Bucky, his mouth full of pancakes and syrup.

Danny turned one hand palm up and shook his head at Uncle Bucky.

"There's an old bike in the garage," said Uncle Bucky. "I'll check the tires for air and give the gears a little oil."

The bike had a name, Uncle Bucky told Danny.

He clipped the air hose onto the tire and started to pump.

"All bikes need names," he said. "I named this when it was mine."

Danny raised a questioning eyebrow.

"Falcon," said Uncle Bucky, laughing. "Like the Millennium Falcon?"

Danny smiled and nodded.

"It's yours now, so you name it."

Danny thought a moment. Not "Star Wars"—Uncle Bucky already did that.

Something that sounds fast, really fast. Maybe Lightning. Or Speedy. Or Streaky. Or…

Danny grabbed a stick and wrote the name in the sand outside the garage. Uncle Bucky leaned over the bike to read it.

"Genie?"

Danny nodded.

"Genie?" asked Uncle Bucky. "Now, how did *that* name come into your head?

Danny shrugged his shoulders.

"Now, that's an unusual name. For a bike. For a person. For anything." Uncle Bucky unclipped the air hose and squeezed the front tire. "But it's your bike. Your bike, your name."

Uncle Bucky took his hands off the handlebars. "Here you go, young man."

Danny set off on the bike along the path to Miss Sally's.

He had a five-dollar bill from Gramps in his pocket. That should be enough for the new issue of *Adventure Time* plus licorice and maybe a candy bar. Or jelly beans. Or gummy bears.

It sure went faster on a bike than on foot, Danny thought. The little bumps and curves of the path that he hardly noticed on foot were exciting on a bike. He was at Miss Sally's in no time.

There were already three bikes leaning outside the store. A big, black 10-speed. A flashy red road bike. And a pink bicycle with a basket on the front.

The door to Miss Sally's slammed and out walked Michael, Aaron, and Lily.

"Oh, great," said Aaron. "The dummy."

Miss Sally's quavering voice called out from inside the store. "He's not stupid! He's just silent!"

Lily laughed and rolled her eyes.

"Hey, Danny," she said. She stood her bike up and set a small bag in the basket. "My little sister's bike," she said to Danny. She made a disgusted face. "*My* bike has a flat tire."

Michael nodded to Danny. "Lily has the coolest bike of all."

"It's fastest," said Aaron.

"You mean, *I'm* fastest," said Lily. "I have to get this back to Mom before lunch. Bye, guys!" Lily rode off.

"Cornmeal," said Michael. "Her mom's making catfish."

Danny nodded.

"You got a bike, I see," said Michael.

"Looks old," said Aaron, with a sneer.

"Vintage," said Michael. "Cool."

"Let's see if you can keep up," said Aaron.

They rode hard and fast. Danny's legs pumped to keep up. It was hard to keep pumping so fast, and the muscles in his legs started to ache. It was hard, but it was fun, too.

At first, he just followed Michael, who followed Aaron, and Danny didn't pay attention to where they were going. But soon, he started noticing new things. New shops and houses he and Gramps had never walked past. New roads he and Uncle Bucky had never driven on in Gramps's car.

Up ahead, Aaron took a sharp right turn off the road and into the woods. Michael followed. It looked as if the trees and undergrowth had swallowed up both boys. It made Danny a little nervous, but he plunged in right after them anyway.

There was a path, though it was hard to see from the road. The woods here were deeper and darker than the woods along the path from Gramps's house to Miss Sally's store.

The tree branches reached lower and lower. Michael, on the tallest bike, had to duck down so branches wouldn't scrape his face.

Vines and plants grew close to the path and caught on Danny's legs and in the bike wheels. Aaron yelped and his bike suddenly wavered. "Poison ivy!" he yelled, and Michael and Danny both lifted their legs high into the air and let the bikes coast past the ivy.

The woods got even darker. Suddenly, Danny saw little points of light dancing along the sides of the path. One or two darted across in front of his bike.

"Lightning bugs!" Michael yelled back over his shoulder. "They think it's night!"

Danny was starting to think it was night, too, although he knew it wasn't even lunchtime yet.

He could hear Michael and Aaron having an argument up ahead of him, but he couldn't make out all of the words.

"—don't, man!" yelled Michael.

Aaron said something that ended with "—chicken!"

Danny heard the squeak and squeal of the hand brakes on Aaron's bike. Danny stopped pedaling and slammed on his brakes, too. The bikes kicked up a cloud of dust and, for a moment, Danny couldn't see where they were.

It was a house. Or a shop. Or a house that was a shop.

Two women stood on the porch, chatting. One held a rolled up mat under her arm. The pair looked happy, talking and laughing.

The front door of the house opened. A man walked up to the door from inside the house. His shadow fell on the floorboards of the porch. The women nodded and smiled to him. He held the door open, and they entered the house.

Danny looked over at Aaron and Michael. Aaron was snickering. "Bunch of weirdos."

"Knock it off, Aaron!" whispered Michael.

Danny didn't know what to do. The women didn't look like weirdos. He couldn't see the man, but his shadow didn't look weird. He didn't have horns, or huge, pointy ears, or horse's legs, or anything. Was Aaron just mad at everyone or did he have some reason for calling the ladies weirdos?

Aaron took off on his bike.

Michael looked a little embarrassed, but he hopped up on his seat and started pedaling, too.

As Danny grabbed the handlebars of his bike, he heard a quiet voice from just behind the door of the little house. It didn't sound weird at all. It actually sounded kind.

"When the time is right, young one," the man's voice said. "When the time is right!"

Danny followed the bikes ahead of him until they reached a fork in the path.

He knew this place.

Danny looked around him. Yes, this was familiar. He was facing from a new direction, but he knew where he was. There was the path to Gramps's house. There was the path to Miss Sally's. He and Aaron and Michael had been on the Secret Path!

"Know where you are, dummy?" asked Aaron.

"Shut up, Aaron," said Michael. He turned to Danny. "That's the path to your Grandpa's, right?"

Danny nodded.

"I have to get home to babysit my sister," said Michael. "And Aaron has something impossibly cool to do, I'm sure."

Danny didn't laugh out loud, but his eyes twinkled. Michael smiled at Aaron.

"See ya!" Michael yelled over his shoulder.

And they were off.

# chapter ELEVEN

**D**anny loved the Visiting Dad space that Gramps had built for him in the old shed.

He loved the old flannel shirt that Dad used to wear. He loved the old photographs of Dad growing up. He loved reading Dad's favorite book. He loved just rocking in that small rocking chair, thinking of nothing in particular.

Gramps had been right. When Danny sat in the rocking chair in that shed, he felt like he was close to Dad. Danny had worried about how he would travel to the cemetery and be close to Dad. Danny was relieved that he felt Dad all around him, here.

Here, and in his dreams.

Every night now, Danny went to sleep eagerly. He knew he would see Dad in his dreams. Each night, they worked on building the walls of Danny's fortress higher and wider. Dad whistled, and Danny brought him stones to set into the wall. Sometimes they talked.

"What do you suppose these stones are made out of?" asked Dad one night.

"I dunno," said Danny.

"Well, think about it, son," said Dad. "You want to make yourself feel safe from what scares you. So what do you build your safe place out of?"

Danny thought and thought. "I still don't know," he said.

"I think you do," said Dad. "Where do you feel safe?"

Danny knew the answer to that one. "In the shed Gramps made for me," he said.

"Good," said Dad. "And where else?"

"Home, with Mom," said Danny.

"Good again," said Dad. "You feel safe when you think of people who love you. You feel safe when you remember people you loved. Good stones to build a fortress out of—use those."

Dad handed Danny a big, grey stone, and Danny set it into the wall.

"Here's another kind of stone," said Dad, reaching for a reddish, smaller one. "When people you love can't be around, you can take care of yourself. This is a taking-care-of-yourself stone."

Danny took the stone from Dad. "I can do that," said Danny.

"I know you can, son," said Dad. "One more kind of stone." He handed Danny a black, shiny stone. "A very strong stone. This one isn't about feeling. This one is about thinking. When you are afraid, you stop and think. Think about what scares you. Why does it scare you? Why are you afraid? That gives you the key to making yourself *not* afraid."

"A thinking stone," said Danny.

"A thinking stone," said Dad. "You stop and think. Even when you're scared, you stop and think."

Danny nodded. "Stop and think."

"You have a good mind, little man," said Dad. "You remember to use it, now."

As they built the walls of Danny's fortress, they could hear the tiger growling and pacing off in the woods. It sounded just as big and scary as ever. But it stayed in the woods. It was as if he was waiting for Dad to leave, Danny thought. Then the tiger will get me alone. That's why it's waiting.

Then one night, Danny dreamed a sad and different dream.

He and Dad were on tall ladders, working at the very top of the walls of the fortress. They were setting the final row of stones in place.

Dad stopped whistling for a moment to talk. "You know," he said. "We'll be done with this fortress of yours tonight."

"Tonight?" asked Danny. "Great! Then we can sit inside the fortress and draw, and play games, and…"

"No, son," said Dad, gently. "When we finish building this fort for you, I'll be leaving."

"No!" yelled Danny. The ladder he was standing on shook as he yelled. He started to cry. "I like seeing you when I dream. Don't leave, Dad! Don't leave!"

"Let's climb down the ladders," said Dad. Dad backed down from the top of the wall, holding on to the ladder with both hands, placing his feet carefully on one rung after the other. Danny watched him, and then did exactly what Dad did.

"See how that worked?" said Dad. "I show you how, and you learn. Remember that. Along the way, lots of people will show you how to do one thing or another. It's smart of you to pay attention. Learn from them."

Now Dad set both his hands on both of Danny's shoulders.

"This is hard, and it's grown-up stuff," said Dad. "Listening?"

Danny wiped his eyes with his sleeve. He felt mad and sad at the same time.

"You need my help for a while," said Dad. "But not forever."

"No, Dad, no—I *need* you forever!"

"You said you'd listen, little man. Now try hard."

Danny sniffed and said in a small voice, "Okay."

"I helped as long as I could," said Dad. "Do I want to be here with you, still helping? Yes, of course. Do I want to be home with you and your Mother? Of course I do. But I can't, and that's the way it is for us."

Danny wanted to cry and cry. But he tried to keep listening, because he promised Dad that he would.

"We built a fine, strong fortress together. You come here anytime that old tiger is trying to bother you."

"I will," said Danny.

"And the next time you need to feel safe, you remember what I taught you. You remember how strong you really are," said Dad. "That's one way of keeping me with you."

"I will," said Danny.

"You tell your mother I love her," said Dad.

Danny nodded.

And Dad was gone.

"No pancakes this morning?" asked Gramps.

Danny shook his head.

"Orange juice?" asked Uncle Bucky.

Danny folded his arms on the table and set his head down on them.

Gramps and Uncle Bucky looked at each other.

Gramps dug into his pants pocket. "Got five dollars here for a trip to Miss Sally's." He set the bill down at Danny's plate. Danny didn't even look up.

"Those buddies of yours will be riding their bikes there this morning, sure as anything," said Gramps. "I'll water the tomatoes myself today. You go on and have some fun."

Head still down, Danny shook his head no.

Gramps and Uncle Bucky looked at each other again.

"Want to talk, little man?" asked Uncle Bucky.

Danny shook his head again.

Silence at the breakfast table.

Finally, Gramps said something odd.

"You know, Grandson," he said, in a quiet-for-Gramps voice. "That path leads somewhere other than off to Miss Sally's."

Uncle Bucky looked puzzled. Gramps gave Uncle Bucky a wink.

Uncle Bucky pushed back his chair and followed Gramps out of the kitchen.

Danny sat there alone at the table. What did Gramps mean? That path leads somewhere else? Where could—?

Then, a little voice in Danny's head said: "Aha!"

Danny rode his bike to the fork in the path.

He turned right and took the Secret Path.

The woods got dark again. And darker.

Trees and plants brushed the handlebars of Danny's bicycle.

Sparkles of lightning bugs danced on both sides of the path.

It was as if the little dots of light were leading him right to the little house in the woods where Aaron thought the weirdos gathered.

A cloud of lightning bugs, like fairies holding lanterns, gathered around the house's front door.

As Danny set the bike down gently in the damp grass, the door opened.

And there was Uncle Bucky, looking unsurprised.

"Come in, young one," he said. "I have been waiting for you."

The door opened into one very large room, with almost no furniture in it.

A stool with no back sat in a corner.

A fireplace on one wall was cold on this warm morning. In front of it sat two small, thick rugs.

The floor was polished wood, gleaming and spotless.

Uncle Bucky looked down at Danny's sneakers. Danny looked down, too, and saw that Uncle Bucky was barefoot. Danny bent down and untied his shoes.

Uncle Bucky smiled, and the lines around his kind eyes and warm smile deepened.

"Come," he said.

Danny followed him.

"Sit." Uncle Bucky settled himself on one of the rugs.

Danny squatted and sat.

"Try this," said Uncle Bucky. "See if it is comfortable."

Danny looked at how Uncle Bucky arranged his legs, bent at the knee and crossed at the ankle. He tried it. He didn't know if he could sit like this for hours, but it was okay for a few minutes.

Uncle Bucky did not ask Danny why he was on the Secret Path in the woods. He did not give Danny a job to do. He did not ask Danny questions. Uncle Bucky did not say anything a regular adult would say. Instead, he opened his arms wide and said, "Let us see if we can quiet your mind."

I didn't know my mind was noisy, thought Danny. But Uncle Bucky knew things Danny didn't always know, like what his dad's funeral would be like, and how Danny would feel about all the people asking questions. Maybe Uncle Bucky could hear a noisy mind, thought Danny.

So Danny just nodded.

"Meditation," said Uncle Bucky.

Meditation? Thought Danny.

"Meditation," said Uncle Bucky. "Close your eyes. Just be here, for a little while."

Danny didn't know how to be anywhere else but here, so he figured that part was easy. And he could close his eyes. So he did as Uncle Bucky told him.

"Silence," said Uncle Bucky. "A good thing."

Well, I specialize in that, thought Danny, and laughed to himself. Oops! He thought. Maybe laughing makes my mind noisy.

"Of course you are always breathing," said Uncle Bucky. "But now, try thinking about your breathing. Make your breathing like music. Let it have a steady beat."

Danny thought about his breathing. He wasn't sure how to breathe in a steady beat. He wasn't sure how to make his breathing like music. He thought of the one song he could play on the piano at RJ's house: "Old McDonald." He tried to breathe in time to the music. Breathe in: *Old McDonald had a farm.* Breathe out: *Ee eye ee eye oh.* Maybe that was how to make his breathing like music.

"Ah, good," said Uncle Bucky. "Nice and steady. Now can you think just about the breathing?"

That's what I *was* doing, though Danny.

"Try to let go of thinking about Gramps. Let go of thinking about the bike, and the path, and the boys who ride bikes with you."

Hm, thought Danny. I guess I was thinking a little about those things.

"Right now, just for a few minutes, you don't need to think about school, or homeroom, or your friends, or your school work. Just give yourself a few minutes of thinking of…nothing."

I don't know how to think of nothing, Danny thought. Do I think of a big, black nothingness? Do I think of everything, and then try to think the opposite? How do I do it?

"You'll know how," said Uncle Bucky. "Trust yourself."

And so Danny tried to sit still, and let his mind be still. He tried to not imagine about what Fish and RJ and Shawn were doing back home. He tried to not worry if Mom was lonesome without him there. He tried to not wonder how it was that Dad was killed in Afghanistan.

He tried to not think about falling asleep tonight knowing he would not see Dad in his dream.

That didn't work. Just having that thought upset Danny. He lost track of his breathing.

"Your mind is used to being noisy," said Uncle Bucky. "You have things to think about. Fine. Think about them. But not at this time. For right now, for just this moment, breathe and be."

Danny started again. Breathe in: *Old McDonald had a farm.* Breathe out: *Ee eye ee eye oh.* I'll think about Dad, but later. I'll think about school, but later. I'll think about—football! I wonder if I'll be back home in time for football!

"Quiet mind," reminded Uncle Bucky. "Breathe and be."

I'll think about football—later, thought Danny. Breathe and be. Breathe and be. It felt nice. It did feel quieter in his mind. Danny felt his shoulders relax, and he hadn't known they were tight. Danny's arms felt heavier, and heavier. His hands rested on his knees. He breathed in. He breathed out. It felt good to not have to think about everything all at the same time.

Danny heard a gentle rustling, and felt the floor boards shift and heard them creak.

"Enough for today," said Uncle Bucky.

Danny opened his eyes. Uncle Bucky was standing. "You were brave today," he said.

Me, brave? Thought Danny. All I did was breathe.

Danny stood up, too. Uncle Bucky isn't a weirdo, but this house is sort of weird. Uncle Bucky lives at Gramps's house, but comes here to the woods to a house with no furniture in it. Not even a lamp. And here, he just sits around and breathes.

"Let me give you something to help you," said Uncle Bucky. He walked to the fireplace and reached up to the mantel. He pulled down a small golden object. He held it out to Danny.

A lamp! A lamp shaped like Aladdin's lamp in the picture in Dad's favorite book, low and curvy. A lamp that looked a little like the gravy pitcher Mom used at Thanksgiving. A lamp like in my dream.

"Before you sleep, meditate on the lamp," said Uncle Bucky. "Try to see it, and nothing else. It will help quiet your mind." Uncle Bucky placed the lamp in Danny's hands. "And give you sweet dreams."

Danny scribbled the question on a pad of paper and passed it to Gramps, who sat on the porch drinking his sweet tea.

Gramps read the paper. Danny thought he saw Gramps's eyes crinkle a little bit, like they did just before he smiled. But there was no smile. Now Gramps looked serious.

"Did your father ever do yoga?" asked Gramps.

Danny nodded.

"Well," said Gramps. "Meditation is a little like yoga. In yoga, you put your body in all sorts of positions. In meditation, you just sit or lie in one position for the whole time."

Danny grabbed back the pad, scribbled letters onto it, and passed it back to Gramps.

Gramps took the pad, read it, and took a sip of his sweet tea. "'How long?' Hm...well, even a few minutes does you good." He set his tea down on the porch table.

"You know, lots of athletes do this," he said. "They say it helps them focus on the game. It helps them do their best."

Danny looked surprised.

"Oh, yes sir," said Gramps. "P.J. Daniels and Ricky Williams, who both played for the Baltimore Ravens. One of the greatest coaches in the history of the National Basketball Association, Phil Jackson. Joe Namath. Arthur Ashe, Jr., the tennis guy? Olympic athletes, college athletes. Lots of famous people meditate, too."

Danny smiled.

"I suppose it's a little like praying, too," said Gramps. "It's not a religion, it's not a religious thing. But some people pray by getting quiet in their heads, and that's sort of what meditation is like."

Gramps poured himself another glass of tea. He offered the pitcher to Danny, but Danny shook his head no. Gramps picked a snip of mint from the bowl and added it to his tea. "You know," he said, with a twinkle in his eye, "if meditating before bed will keep you quiet all night, I'm all for it!"

Danny snatched the pad back and wrote a question on it for Gramps.

Gramps read over Danny's shoulder. "'Why don't *I* meditate?'" Gramps gave Danny a playful punch on the shoulder. "How do you know I don't, little man?"

Danny brushed his teeth. He put on his pajamas. He said his prayers. When he prayed for Dad, he thought, "Dad, I'm going to try to meditate. So for a few minutes, I won't be thinking about you. I still miss you and love you, and I'll start thinking about you again as soon as I'm done."

Then he reached under his bed and pulled out the lamp Uncle Bucky had given him. He climbed up on the bed and tried to sit in the cross-legged position Uncle Bucky showed him. He set the lamp on the bed in front of him.

Maybe like Aladdin's lamp, this one had a genie in it. Maybe if Danny rubbed it, the genie would pop out and give him three wishes! Danny knew what Wish Number One would be: Bring Dad back. That would be real magic. And probably impossible, even for a genie. But Danny could wish it, anyway.

Wish Number Two? Make me talk again. It would be nice to be able to ask Gramps if he wanted more sweet tea, rather than walk over to him and point to the tea. It would be nice to tell Uncle Bucky about how Dad helped build the dream fortress, instead of having to write out words on a pad. Danny couldn't write the words fast enough to feel like he was really talking with someone.

Wish Number Three? Maybe that Lily would smile at him again. She had a pretty smile. Maybe that Uncle Bucky's bike had a new seat. That old one was hard and worn out, with leather curling up on the edges. Maybe that Gramps's pancakes were just a little less runny in the middle. Danny could eat around the edges, but Gramps was starting to suspect why Danny never ate the middles.

He thought about rubbing the lamp to see what would happen. But then he thought that was silly.

So he focused on the lamp. And tried to breathe and be.

# chapter TWELVE

D anny dreamt of the fortress.

It stood in the grass, just where he and Dad had built it. It looked strong and fine. Danny was proud that he helped built it.

He walked up to the door and it opened.

Mr. Fishman was standing inside.

"Mr. Fishman!" said Danny. "What are you doing here?"

"Why, hello, Danny," said Mr. Fishman. "I was just making a lamp delivery."

Mr. Fishman handed Danny a lamp that looked just like the lamp Uncle Bucky had given him. "Remember this, Danny: Lamps can guide you even when their light is not turned on."

Then Mr. Fishman walked out of the fortress and off into the woods.

"Watch out for the tiger!" yelled Danny.

Mr. Fishman turned around and waved. "Tigers never bother me!" he laughed, and kept on walking.

Danny locked the fortress door behind him and set the lamp down on the floor inside. He didn't remember building a floor with Dad, but there was one there, anyway.

Then, the tiger roared.

The tiger roared so loudly that the walls shook. The floor shook. And Danny's hands shook, too.

He must be right outside the door to be that loud, thought Danny. Right there! I hope that lock holds!

Then Danny remembered what to do.

He remembered that Dad told him to remember his own strength. So Danny thought about that. That Aaron guy tries to make me mad every time I see him, and I don't let him bother me, thought Danny. Maybe that's being strong. I traveled all the way to Mississippi and am far away from my friends and my school, thought Danny. Maybe that's being strong. And every day, I wake up sad that I am missing my dad, but I still get out of bed. I know that's being strong because that's really hard to do. I can be strong.

He remembered that Uncle Bucky said, "Trust yourself. You'll know how."

He remembered Gramps calling the shed a "sit and think place. Your dad is not so far away here."

And Mr. Fishman had said, "Lamps can guide you, even when they're not turned on."

The tiger roared outside. Danny took a deep breath and sat down in front of the lamp. "I can be strong," he told himself. "I can trust myself. And Dad is not so far away." He breathed in and out, in and out. The lamp helped him. It gave him something to look at. It helped him see inside himself.

The tiger's roar got quieter.

"The lamp is helping," said Uncle Bucky, the next time he and Danny were meditating together. "Your focus has improved this week. You can meditate for 10 minutes, now, before you start to squirm."

Danny smiled. Uncle Bucky was right. The lamp was helping. The lamp was starting to feel like Danny's meditating friend. Danny imagined the lamp knew just how to meditate, and helped Danny do it. Sometimes, Danny imagined the lamp did have a genie in it—a secret genie that didn't show itself or speak but who still granted secret wishes.

"You might notice your body working better," said Uncle Bucky. "You might notice your thoughts working better."

Danny nodded. He wrote words on a pad of paper.

"Ah!" Uncle Bucky smiled as he read the pad. "'The tiger roars more quietly now.' As it should. As it should."

At the door, Danny put on his shoes. Uncle Bucky handed him the lamp. "We'll try 15 minutes tomorrow."

Danny smiled as Uncle Bucky closed the door. He had been meditating with Uncle Bucky for two weeks. Dad wasn't in his dreams, and Danny missed that. But the tiger was less scary, and that was a good thing.

The lamp swung back and forth on the handlebars of Genie, the bicycle.

Danny had put it inside a plastic grocery bag and tied it on tight. The bumps and curves of the path to Gramps's house from Uncle Bucky's meditation house made the bag swing, but the knot was tight and the lamp was safe.

Danny heard it before he saw it. The squeaky brakes of Aaron's bike made noise before Aaron and the bike squealed around the corner and stopped in a cloud of dust. Danny slammed on his brakes. He stopped inches from Aaron's bike.

"Hey, dummy!" said Aaron. "Visiting the crazy old man?"

Danny froze.

"Can't you talk at all, dummy?" Aaron laughed.

Danny wondered what to do. He couldn't ride past Aaron; the path was too narrow. He didn't think he could fight Aaron and win. Danny hadn't been in an actual fight, but he had seen them on movies and on TV. Maybe he could try a cool Iron Man move. But he didn't have the magical suit. So he would just end up with a bloody nose or a loose tooth or something gross like that. Or, he could turn around and ride really fast to Uncle Bucky's house. That might work.

Danny gripped the handlebars tighter and got ready to turn the bike around.

Suddenly, Aaron reached out and ripped the plastic bag holding the lamp off Danny's bike. "What's this, dummy?"

Aaron ripped the bag open.

"Aladdin's lamp!" he sneered. "Just what a freak like you would carry around."

Then Aaron turned his bike around in a flash and took off with the lamp.

The lamp!

Danny had lost the lamp!

Danny hopped back onto his bicycle's seat and pushed the pedals hard. He pedaled as fast as he could.

He imagined the bike flying down the path toward Gramps's house.

He could see Aaron up ahead, but Aaron's bike had gears and faster speeds and Uncle Bucky's old bike ran only on leg power. And Danny's legs were getting tired.

Aaron raced past the fork in the path but did not turn right and head up to Miss Sally's toward his house. Maybe Aaron didn't mean to do that, thought Danny. He probably wanted to head home but didn't see the turn through all the dust he's raising. Or maybe he just forgot to turn because he was too busy trying to go fast and faster.

Because Aaron didn't seem to realize he was headed straight for Gramps's house. Maybe Uncle Bucky would be out back, washing the car, and would stop Aaron and save the lamp, thought Danny. Maybe Gramps would be watering the tomatoes and turn the hose on Aaron. The thought of Aaron getting blasted with water and heading home dripping wet made Danny smile.

Just up ahead now, almost to Gramps's back yard.

Danny could just see the edge of the garage. He could just start to make out the tomatoes, staked and starting to redden. Sure enough, there was Gramps, walking out of the shed! And there was Uncle Bucky, right behind him! Maybe they were having a "sit and think" time about Dad, just like Danny liked to do. Gramps was still holding the door to the shed open. And there was—

"Mom!" yelled Danny.

The sound made Aaron stop his bike. He turned around to face Danny. Aaron's mouth was a big "O" of surprise.

That might have made Danny laugh, except that there was Mom, standing with Gramps and Uncle Bucky, her arms held out wide, tears on her cheeks.

Danny dropped his bike in the path and ran to her.

"Mom!" Danny said, over and over again. "Mom, Mom, Mom, Mom, Mom." Her dress was soft and smelled like flowers.

Gramps set his hand on Danny's head. Danny heard Gramps clear his throat.

"You talked, little dude!" yelled Uncle Bucky.

"Not so loud, son!" boomed Gramps. Uncle Bucky looked at Danny and winked.

"Stand back and let me look at you," said Mom. "You're so tall."

Don't cry, Mom, Danny thought. Then he tried to say it. "Do—Don't—" He put his hand up to his throat.

"Give yourself a minute, there, Grandson," said Gramps. "You've been quiet a long time."

Mom kissed the top of Danny's head. Then she kissed his nose. Then she kissed each cheek. "Have you been feeding him?" she teased Gramps. "He looks so thin!"

"The boy eats, Gwen, believe me," said Gramps.

Mom looked over the top of Danny's head. "Where did your friend go?"

Danny looked up at her, puzzled. His friend? Oh, Aaron!

Danny shook his head. "Not…my friend," he said.

"Into the house," said Gramps, in his big, loud voice. "Out of the afternoon sun. Bucky—tea!"

Danny liked listening to the grown-ups talk.

He rested his head on Mom's shoulder. She spoke now and then, in a soft kind of murmur. Gramps boomed away, but sometimes, especially when he spoke about Dad, his voice got softer. Uncle Bucky laughed sometimes, and sometimes he sounded sad. Listening made Danny feel safe and warm. The three of them made a kind of music together.

Danny wondered if he could meditate to that. Breathe in: *murmur boom laugh*. Breathe out: *laugh boom murmur*. He might try that tonight. But he wouldn't have the lamp. Would he still be able to meditate?

"Did Dad meditate?" asked Danny.

Mom smiled and stroked Danny's hair. It was so good to hear his voice. "Yes, sometimes," she said. "He said it helped him focus on his drawing." She looked thoughtfully into Danny's eyes. "Have you been meditating?"

Danny hoped it would be okay with Mom. He nodded. "I think...it makes the tiger go away."

"No more bad dreams?" Mom looked up at Gramps, then Uncle Bucky.

Uncle Bucky grinned. "The kid hasn't screamed me awake for days."

Mom hugged Danny. "That is great news!"

"Something else," said Danny. "Dad stopped visiting me in my dreams."

Mom looked sad. "Oh, honey," she said.

"It's kinda okay," said Danny. "I know what to do now." Mom hugged him tighter. "And Mom?"

"What, baby?"

"Dad says he loves you."

Mom kissed the top of Danny's head and said nothing.

Danny sat on his bed and stared at the spot where the lamp used to sit.

Maybe if I focus on that seam in the bedspread, he thought. Maybe if I focus on that piece of lint on the blanket.

He tried to breathe and be but it just wasn't working.

That worried Danny. He liked meditating. He liked being still and feeling focused. He liked not worrying and not feeling tense. He liked what Uncle Bucky called his "quiet mind." Now that the lamp was gone, would his mind always be noisy?

Danny dreamt of the tiger.

It roared and roared.

Danny cowered and hid inside the walls of the fortress.

Outside, the tiger snarled and growled. Its roars got louder and louder. The walls shook. And then the tiger jumped against the wall of the fortress, dug in its claws, and started to climb.

Danny screamed.

# chapter THIRTEEN

*M*om's pancakes were better than Gramps's pancakes. Hers weren't runny in the middle.

Uncle Bucky noticed, too. Danny could tell, because Uncle Bucky ate six pancakes, instead of five.

Gramps stood next to Mom at the stove, making bacon.

Everyone had heard him scream last night. Danny knew it. Gramps knew it. Mom knew it. Uncle Bucky knew it.

But no one said anything.

Danny felt embarrassed. He had bragged about his dreams getting better, and then—bang! He had the worst nightmare of all. He felt like he had done something wrong.

Mom brought more pancakes to the table. For no reason, she reached out and held Danny's hand for a moment. He wished she hadn't done that. Now he felt really embarrassed.

There was a knock at the front door.

Gramps went to answer it. Uncle Bucky, curious, got up, too. Mom looked at Danny and shrugged.

In a minute, Gramps and Uncle Bucky came back into the kitchen.

"It's for you, Grandson," said Gramps. "Your friend."

Friend? Thought Danny.

"Aaron," said Uncle Bucky.

Aaron sat in the living room, the lamp on his knees. He looked unhappy and nervous.

That was interesting, thought Danny. He had seen Aaron look crabby and angry, but he had never seen him look unhappy and nervous.

Danny raised a hand and waved. "Hi," he said.

"My mom made me come," said Aaron. "I guess you're not a dummy." Then he winced. "That didn't come out right."

"I guess not," said Danny. He sat down on a chair opposite Aaron.

Aaron picked up the lamp and held it out to Danny. "I brought your lamp back."

"Thanks," said Danny, taking the lamp. "Why?"

Aaron looked at his feet. He squirmed a little on the sofa.

"That sofa is kinda lumpy," said Danny.

Aaron smiled a little. "Yeah. It is."

Danny waited.

Aaron looked at the ceiling. "That was dumb," Aaron said.

Danny was surprised. "What was dumb?"

"I was dumb," said Aaron. "Taking the lamp was dumb. Calling you a dummy was dumb."

Danny felt even more surprised.

"I shouldn't have done that," said Aaron.

Aaron had been nothing but mean to Danny. Danny could not imagine why Aaron was now being kind. But for some reason, Danny wanted to make Aaron feel better. Danny didn't like to see Aaron feel so uncomfortable.

"It's okay," said Danny. "I'm glad to have the lamp back. I missed it."

"It's a cool lamp," said Aaron.

Danny nodded.

"How's it work?" asked Aaron.

"You mean, does a genie come out if you rub it?" asked Danny.

Aaron laughed a little and moved closed to the lamp. "Yeah."

"No genie," said Danny. "It doesn't really do anything." But then Danny remembered what Mr. Fishman said. "But lamps can guide you, even when their lights are not turned on."

Aaron nodded, as if he understood that. Then he said, "I don't get that."

Danny laughed. "Sometimes I don't get that, either." They both started laughing.

"My dad left," said Aaron. "My dad just left. When I was five. I don't know why."

"I'm sorry, man," said Danny.

"Yeah," said Aaron.

The two boys sat there a while in silence.

Gramps, Mom, and Uncle Bucky sat around the kitchen table.

Uncle Bucky started on his seventh pancake.

Mom was picking at hers.

Gramps was sipping his third cup of coffee.

Suddenly, he stopped. "Hear that?" he asked.

"Hear what?" asked Uncle Bucky.

Mom moved to the back window. "Well," she said in amazement. "Will you look at that?"

Uncle Bucky and Gramps pushed back their chairs and came to the window, too. Out in the back yard, between the tomatoes and the little shed, Danny and Aaron were playing catch. The ball made a *thunk* sound each time it hit their mitts.

"Will wonders never cease?" said Gramps.

When it was time for Aaron to go home, he picked up his bike and waved goodbye to Danny. Something about Aaron's shoulders looked small and sad to Danny. Then he had a thought. It was a thought that started with Dad and Gramps and then came through Mr. Fishman and Ms. Albright and then through Uncle Bucky and Mom. And, it came through the tiger, too, because the tiger taught Danny what it was like to feel really scared and not very strong.

"Wait," said Danny. "Wait."

He walked over to Aaron. "Here," said Danny. "You take the lamp."

Aaron looked surprised. "Me? Why give it to me?"

Danny shrugged. "I dunno," he said. "I just think it's yours now."

Aaron looked at the lamp in his hand. Danny could tell Aaron liked it—a lot. Aaron set the lamp in the basket on the back wheel of his bike.

"I'll take good care of it," he said to Danny.

"Good," said Danny.

Aaron turned his bike around and swung his leg over the bar. "Hey," he called to Danny. "You wanna ride to Miss Sally's tomorrow?"

Danny smiled. "Sure," he said.

Aaron smiled, too. "You can get one of those stupid comic books you like so much!"

Danny laughed and waved.

Aaron rode off.

The lamp clanked noisily in the basket on the bike.

I wonder what Aaron named *his* bike, Danny thought.

That night, Danny dreamt of the fortress again.

But this time, he didn't walk through the fortress front door. He didn't go inside. The stars in the night sky looked so pretty. The breeze was so balmy. The grass was so cool. So Danny just sat down in the grass and leaned back against the wall of the fortress.

He thought about the lamp. He thought there wasn't a genie in that old lamp, but maybe there had been. Because something almost magical had happened. He had learned to help himself not be so scared. Of Aaron. Of being without Dad. Of saying the wrong thing. Of tigers.

He knew the tiger was out there.

He could hear its wet breathing, its noisy panting.

The tiger probably had a tiger path through those woods, only it didn't go to Miss Sally's or to Gramps's house. Maybe its path led right here, to Danny's fortress.

He could hear the tiger moving now. Coming closer. Closer.

There! In the trees!

Moonlight shone off its big teeth. Its striped face was almost hidden in the shadows of the trees.

The tiger growled a little growl.

Danny opened his mouth and growled back, a big growl, a loud growl, but a sort of friendly growl.

The tiger crept out of the woods. It wasn't running. It wasn't snarling. It wasn't so scary, after all.

The tiger padded slowly over to Danny, and sat down with him in the cool, tall grass. And put its head in Danny's lap.

# chapter FOURTEEN

It was hard to catch up in school, but Mom was helping. RJ helped, too, coming over to do homework before dinnertime.

Everyone was being extra nice to him.

Shawn shared his ketchup-covered tater tots at lunch. The first day Danny was back, Twigs shouted "Hey, Danny!" so loud that Danny thought of Gramps and his big, booming voice. And Juliet Browne had smiled at him, smiled with those pretty dimples, and actually said, "We missed you, Danny." *That* was a good day!

It was too late to join the football team. But the coach was Mr. Moore, RJ's homeroom teacher, and he let Danny be a junior manager. "It's your job to help the team focus," said Mr. Moore. So Danny was teaching them a little bit about breathing and being still.

In English class, Ms. Frank asked the class to each write an essay.

"This should be your very best work," she said. "I want you to think hard and really challenge yourselves to write something that matters to you."

"What do we write about?" RJ had asked.

"The hardest thing you've ever had to do," said Ms. Frank.

All the way home on the bus, the kids talked about the essay.

"Thinking of what to write about is the hardest thing I've ever done!" yelled Twigs.

"Learning how to play the cello was tough," said RJ, thoughtfully. "Maybe I'll write about that."

"I don't like cleaning my room," said Shawn.

RJ punched him in the arm. "Don't write about that, you goof!"

Danny didn't say anything. He couldn't wait until he got home and got to work. Already, he could see the story unfolding in his mind. He would sit down at the kitchen table. He would take a fresh piece of paper out of his backpack, and his favorite pen. Mom would bring him a glass of milk. And then he would start writing.

"I used to be afraid of a tiger…"

# acknowledgements

*F*irst, thank you to the Creator.

Thank you to my family: My mother and pops, JoAnn and Steven. My brother and sister, Manjah and Chanitha—the best siblings in the world. All of my uncles who have been very instrumental in my life—Tim, Curtis, Julius, and Kent—because of you I always had something to aspire to.

Thank you to all my friends who have supported me—Calvin Johnson Jr., Gerris B-W, Cordara Howard, C. Lott, J. Carter and many more.

Thank you to my nieces and nephews, Yasmin, Shawn K, Ja'Kar & Jaston, and to all the ones abroad, I love you guys.

Thank you to my publishing team: Mike, Pamela and Liza, Siori and Ovi. The universe works in mysterious ways.

Thank you to my manager R. Nsiah. Nothing is impossible unless you believe it is.

With honor and great gratitude I would like to thank my spiritual guide and guru, Rev. Baba Nazirmoreh.

Finally, thanks and honor to my father. Words cannot express how much I miss you and how fortunate I am to have a strong father to aspire towards to help make this world a better place. Thank you. Love is eternal.

*Prince Daniels, Jr.*

The vision of two men, Mike Sager and Prince Daniels, Jr., began this project, and happily, they invited me into it. Prince created the boy who lost his father only to gain a stronger sense of himself through meditation, and Prince's passion to help young people find their inner strength is an inspiration. Mike is the rarest of publishers: he makes writer's dreams possible, whole, and real, and he always honors the words. I am grateful to Army Master Sergeant Mark Harrell, who generously shared his knowledge of Army life at home and overseas, and to Liza Biggers, who painted Danny Yukon's world vividly and with great warmth. And thank you to Gretchen, Christopher, and Ian, who made me an expert on 10-year-olds and who know all about imagining yourself into who you want to be.

*Pamela Hill Nettleton*

# about the authors

## PRINCE DANIELS, JR.

Prince Ahadzie Daniels, Jr is the son of Prince A. Daniels Sr, from Ghana, Africa, and Jo-Ann Keys, from New Orleans, LA. Born in Houston, Texas, he earned his degree in Business Management at the Institute of Georgia Tech and was named to the All-Academic football team, a two-time all-conference tailback and the fourth-leading rusher in Georgia Tech's history with 3,300 yards. In the 2003 Humanitarian Bowl, he ran for 311 yards and 4 touchdowns, a record that stands. Prince was drafted to the National Football League by the Baltimore Ravens in 2006; he retired three years later due to injuries. Today he is a fitness instructor, motivational speaker, and experienced meditation guide. He frequently travels and teaches in Ghana and is pursuing his masters degree in business from the University of San Diego.

## PAMELA HILL NETTLETON

Pamela Hill Nettleton is a writer, editor, playwright, scriptwriter, librettist, professor and author. Twenty-three of her books are in publication—including a biography of Shakespeare and three series of children's books. More than 300 of her award-winning essays and features have appeared in magazines, newspapers, and websites; her video scripts have won more than 11 national awards, and her plays have enjoyed repeated performances. Her doctorate dissertation on post-9/11 television masculinity won the 2010 Kenneth Harwood Outstanding Dissertation Award from the Broadcast Education Association, and she was awarded the 2014 Way Klingler Teaching Enhancement Award at Marquette University.

# about the illustrator

## LIZA BIGGERS

Liza Biggers is a freelance illustrator who grew up in Florida and spent her teens in Ohio. She received her BA at Wright State University in Ohio before moving to New York City. Life experiences and a love of comics has greatly influenced her art. In March 2006, Liza's brother, Ethan, was shot by a sniper in Baghdad and succumbed to his wounds in February 2007 after a long battle. Liza never left his side and served as one of his primary caregivers. This experience led to many projects involving Veterans and their families. Today, Liza still resides in NYC and continues to illustrate.